# SUSAN GATES

# DR FELL'S CABINET OF SMELLS

*Illustrated by Tony Blundell*

**PUFFIN**

PUFFIN BOOKS

Published by the Penguin Group
Penguin Books Ltd, 80 Strand, London WC2R 0RL, England
Penguin Putnam Inc., 375 Hudson Street, New York, New York 10014, USA
Penguin Books Australia Ltd, 250 Camberwell Road, Camberwell, Victoria 3124, Australia
Penguin Books Canada Ltd, 10 Alcorn Avenue, Toronto, Ontario, Canada M4V 3B2
Penguin Books India (P) Ltd, 11 Community Centre, Panchsheel Park,
New Delhi – 110 017, India
Penguin Books (NZ) Ltd, Cnr Rosedale and Airborne Roads, Albany,
Auckland, New Zealand
Penguin Books (South Africa) (Pty) Ltd, 24 Sturdee Avenue, Rosebank 2196, South Africa

Penguin Books Ltd, Registered Offices: 80 Strand, London WC2R 0RL, England

www.penguin.com

First published 2003
1

Set in 14/17 Baskerville MT

Made and printed in England by Clays Ltd, St Ives plc

British Library Cataloguing in Publication Data
A CIP catalogue record for this book is available from the British Library

ISBN 0–141–31515–6

**Susan Gates** says . . . 'I read somewhere that when we're babies we like all smells. We don't think *any* smells are disgusting. We have to be taught that some smells are 'nice' and some 'nasty' – that it's OK to sniff flowers, but not dog poo! But what would happen if we weren't taught that? If we grew up still thinking, like we did when we were babies, that all smells are wonderful and that we're allowed to sniff anything we like?

# **Chapter One**

**K**it checked around. Good, there was nobody to smell him. Even so, he took out his spray can of Gladiator deodorant and gave himself a quick burst, under one armpit.

'Don't get paranoid,' he told himself.

But he couldn't help it. He gave his other armpit a long blast. He carried deodorant with him at all times now. Ever since Laura at school had said, 'You smell.' At first, he couldn't believe she meant him.

He'd said, 'Who smells?'

And she'd said, 'You. *Phew*, you pong! Doesn't he, Sophie?'

Then, somehow, it had spread around the school. Everyone was saying it. Even kids he thought were his friends. 'I don't want to sit next to him, Miss. He smells!'

How could something so stupid be ruining his life? You smell! It was what *little* kids shouted at each other. But it was shocking what power it had to hurt you. And how hard it was to shake off. Just how do you prove you *don't* smell?

He was beginning to think, Maybe I do! And I've never noticed!

Time for another quick squirt of Gladiator. That can must be almost empty by now. He'd have to get a new one. Personal hygiene products were costing him all his pocket money.

He felt really sorry for himself. He'd been stunned by the speed and savagery of their attack. Like sharks scenting blood. He'd never done anything to hurt them, had he?

Except last week, was it Laura who'd held him up in the dinner queue? And had he said, 'Get out of my way, wobble-bum'?

'But that was different,' he told himself. 'That was just a bit of fun!'

So why were all her mates ganging up on him?

Maybe he should have listened to Gran. 'You should watch that smart mouth of yours,' she'd told him. 'One day it'll get you into trouble.'

Well, it had got him here. Slouching along the slummy part of the canal, where Laura and her friends never went. He'd decided to keep a low profile for a while. Maybe, over the summer holidays, they'd find someone else to pick on.

He whopped at some tall purple weeds with a stick. 'It's not fair!'

The canal was full of floating rubbish – bobbing plastic bottles and pizza boxes. A black rat sailed by on half a burger box, captain of his own little ship. He seemed to be steering it with his scaly, pink tail.

This part of town is a real dump, thought Kit.

Old factories and warehouses crammed the canal banks. They'd been empty for years. Bramble bushes swarmed through their smashed windows. Willow trees rooted in their walls.

Kit gave an empty Coke can a vicious kick. He was in a bad mood. He wanted his life back to normal.

'You've got to make that Laura say she

made a mistake. That you *don't* smell,' he said, out loud.

'But you *do* smell,' answered a girl's voice.

*Aaaaargh!* Kit's whole body cringed. He reached for his can of Gladiator.

Who said that? he thought.

How had his stinking reputation spread this far? He was in a strange, forgotten part of town. Miles away from his own neighbourhood.

Then he saw someone, coming out from behind a willow tree. You could hardly miss her. Her lime-green dress was so bright it probably glowed in the dark. It was a tatty old party frock, all frills and sequins.

Kit thought, Did she buy that from a jumble sale?

She had scruffy white trainers on with it. She looked like a ragbag princess. But she was doing something princesses don't usually do.

She's sniffing that tree! thought Kit, horrified.

She was kneeling, sniffing low down. She had her nose really close to the trunk. Her eyes were closed. There was a blissful look on her face. She sniffed a bit more.

'*Ahhh*, Alsatian dog,' she said.

# Chapter Two

'Get out of here fast,' Kit's brain told him. 'This is far too freaky!'

It was creepy too. Seeing a girl sniffing a tree like a wild creature. And, anyway, how did this complete stranger know his shameful secret?

The girl had stopped sniffing. She got up. She was walking towards him! The frills on her tatty green party frock trailed behind her like tentacles.

'Hi, my name's Juniper,' she said.

Kit could have made a smart remark. Like, 'So? What do you want me to do about it?'

But instead he blurted out, 'I sprayed myself all over with Gladiator!' He got out his spray can to prove it.

Juniper frowned. 'What's Gladiator?'

Here was another chance for Kit's sharp

tongue. 'Where've you been living? On Mars?' he could have mocked.

Everyone knew about Gladiator. The great new range of body care for boys. There was shampoo and shower gel. All his mates, even the ones who didn't wash, bought it. You just had to have those cool silver cans on your shelf.

But he found himself giving her a straight answer: 'It's deodorant. So you don't smell.'

'But you *do* smell,' the girl insisted again. 'So give me a whiff of your armpit.'

'*AAAAARGH!*' screamed Kit, inside his head. What was going on here? Maybe she *was* from Mars! Earth girls don't go up to strange boys and ask for a whiff of their armpits! It was horribly embarrassing. Besides, what if Laura was right? What if a whole can of Gladiator couldn't disguise his body odour?

'No way!' Kit clamped his arms to his sides, like chicken wings.

Juniper was equally upset. What's wrong with him? she was wondering. Why won't he share smells? That's not very polite.

And she'd been about to suggest they have a good sniff of each other's trainers.

'I just wanted to see if you really smelled like a gladiator,' she said.

Kit let out a hysterical laugh. He just couldn't stop himself. He was sure now this girl was from another planet. She didn't know the slightest thing about shopping.

'Gladiator's just a cool name,' he explained, showing her the can. 'It doesn't mean you *smell* like one. Who'd want to anyway? I bet gladiators smelled of blood and sweat. I bet they smelled like skunks.'

'I bet they didn't,' said Juniper. 'But why not sniff one and see?'

This was too much. Was she making fun of him? 'How can I do that?' he asked her angrily. 'They're all dead, like way back in Roman times.'

But Juniper had drifted off. She was tree-smelling again. She beckoned him over.

'A lot of messages have been left around here,' she said, crouching down.

She took some delicate sniffs at the base of the trunk, as if she was nosing a fine wine.

'I'm smelling golden retriever,' she said. 'It passed this way an hour ago.'

'Are you actually sniffing dog wee?' asked Kit. 'That's disgusting!'

Juniper didn't answer. There was a dreamy look on her face. She pressed her nose to the soil so she could smell better. She slithered along the towpath like a frilly green lizard. Kit shivered. He was starting to find her really sinister. And, besides, the weather was changing. The air felt electric somehow. The purple weeds were rustling. Where had that wind sprung from?

'*Mmmmm*,' said Juniper, as if she'd got a big whiff of the most fabulous smell. Like fresh bread baking, or a bouquet of roses. 'This is Yorkshire terrier, I'd bet you any-thing.'

Kit felt scared and confused. And that made him angry.

'You're making all this up!' he roared. 'What are you trying to say? That you can tell what *kind* of dogs have been here by sniffing their wee?'

Juniper looked surprised. 'Course,' she said coolly, twisting a peppermint-coloured frill round her finger. 'Can't you?'

'No, I can't!'

Poor deprived boy, thought Juniper. That's child cruelty.

Mum had told her about kids like Kit. Kids who'd lost the power of their noses. Kids who'd never learned about the wonderful world of smells. But she'd never met one. She'd hardly met any other kids before. Mum had kept her away from them. In case they passed on their smell prejudice.

'Don't you know,' said Kit, talking very slowly and clearly as if to a very small child, 'that sniffing dog wee is *nasty*? Even boys don't do it. Well, hardly ever. And girls *never* do!'

Especially not girls dressed as princesses.

But Juniper didn't seem at all embarrassed.

'There are no nice and nasty smells!' she retaliated. 'All smells are fascinating! My mum says so. It's just that *your* parents have brainwashed you!'

'No, they haven't!'

'Yes, they have! *Babies* like all smells. Scientists have proved it. Until their parents tell them, "*Phew*, don't sniff that. It's nasty!"'

'For heaven's sake!' Kit had had enough. He spun round to stalk off. How could you argue with a girl as wrong-headed as this one? He didn't know where to start.

'Don't you know you're a freak?' he shouted back at her.

Juniper called after him. 'No, I'm not!'

But her voice was shaky. Kit had touched a nerve. Juniper knew she hadn't been brought up like other children. That she was different. Mum said that made her better than them. But just lately, she'd started to ask herself, 'Will other kids think I'm *weird*?'

All sorts of rubbish ended up here, blown on the wind, carried by the greasy canal. Sometimes, on her sniffing expeditions, Juniper had found scraps of teen magazines. Reading them was a revelation. Their problem pages were full of worries about 'bad' smells. Juniper just couldn't relate to that. She couldn't imagine anyone being ashamed of their own personal smell.

'Hey,' said Kit. He suddenly turned round. He'd been about to make a swift escape. But he had to check something out first.

He went back. 'Hey, why did you say I smelled?'

At least he didn't feel awkward talking

about underarm odours with Juniper. It seemed to be her favourite topic.

'Cos *everyone* does, of course!' explained Juniper. She quoted her mum: 'Your personal smell is a precious gift.'

Kit groaned.

'In Neanderthal times,' Juniper added, 'people smelled really strong. Strong enough to frighten deer away. My mum says so.'

Juniper's mum often talked of Neanderthal times. It was a Golden Age when people really appreciated smells. They had massive hooters for sucking them in. They sniffed each other all over like dogs.

'Neanderthals really knew how to use their noses,' Mum would tell Juniper sadly. 'We modern humans have completely forgotten.'

'You're not saying I smell like a caveman?' Kit felt himself getting insecure again. Where was the nearest shop? He needed a fresh can of Gladiator.

'No. You just smell – like you.'

'So I don't smell like – *Phew!* – you know, horrible?'

Juniper didn't seem to understand the question. 'Be Proud of Your Armpits,' she said, quoting one of her mum's favourite sayings. 'And Cherish your Cheesy Feet.'

Is this kid for real? thought Kit.

Now she was throwing her head back. She was sniffing the air, like a wolf! 'There's bad weather coming,' she said.

Kit could see that for himself. The day had gone dark. The wilderness of wire, weeds and ruined buildings looked more like a wasteland than ever.

'Bye then,' said Juniper.

She stuck a hand out. Kit thought, Does she want me to shake it? But, instead, she snaked her hand up his T-shirt and plunged it into his armpit.

Kit leapt back. 'Gerroff me! What're you doing?'

But then she did something much, much worse. He could hardly believe it. She stroked his armpit smell on to her bare arm and sniffed it.

'Get me out of here!' Kit's brain screamed at him. 'She's a total nutter!'

'What do you think you're doing?' he bellowed again, in shock and outrage.

Juniper took a few steps forward. 'NO, NO!

Don't come near me!' he shrieked. He was  really scared now. Was she some kind of alien life form, who sucked people's brains out through their armpits?

Juniper frowned. What was wrong with this boy? Why was he in such a big panic?

'It's just a friendly farewell,' she said, bewildered by all the fuss. 'When a friend goes away, you keep some of their personal scent. Friends do it all the time in New Guinea. It's no big deal.'

'You're crazy!' shouted Kit, still shaken. 'You can't do that around *here*. Boys will be freaked out! Anyway,' he added, 'I'm not your friend. Right?'

All Juniper's secret fears were confirmed. When she spoke, it was in a hurt little voice. 'Is it because I'm a bit *strange*?' she asked him. 'Is that why you won't be my friend?'

It was the perfect chance for Kit's sharp tongue. He could have hooted with laughter. 'A *bit* strange! You ought to be locked up!' But, for once, he didn't feel like doing that.

'You don't feel *sorry* for her, do you?' the old, sarcastic Kit taunted him. But somewhere, deep inside him, he did. She didn't know how cruel some kids, including him, could be.

'Look, don't you meet other kids at school?' he asked her.

'I don't go to school. Mum teaches me here, at home.'

'Here?' Kit was confused. 'You live here? In this dump?'

'That's our house, number nineteen Canal Street.'

She pointed to a grim, red-brick place, like a prison, right next to the canal. It had rows and rows of windows. It was less tumbledown than the other buildings. But not much. At least trees weren't growing through the walls. And only a few of the windows were smashed.

'What – that big, old factory? You don't live there, do you?'

'Yes, with my mum,' she said. 'She's an expert on smells. She writes books about them.'

That figures, thought Kit, sighing. No wonder this kid was so mixed up. 'Look, you should give up sniffing trees,' he advised her.

'But I've been doing it all my life,' said Juniper. 'It's really interesting. Lots of animals leave scent messages. Did you know bush babies spray the soles of their feet with their own urine and then stamp about to scent-mark their territory?'

'The *soles* of their feet?' repeated Kit, before he could stop himself. 'With their *own* urine? That's clever.'

'Yes, it is,' agreed Juniper. 'I mean, could you do it?'

Kit shook himself hard. It was hopeless. This girl was so far out she'd never fit in with normal kids.

'No, no, no!' he roared, blushing bright pink. 'You don't ask things like that! Us boys are easily embarrassed!'

Juniper never got the chance to reply. Because at that moment the rain came sizzling down. In seconds, the canal was a choppy sea. Had Captain Rat reached shore safely? If not, he wouldn't be afloat much longer. His frail burger boat would be swamped.

Kit hadn't been planning to stay. He felt sorry for Juniper. But what could you do? She could never be allowed out alone. Not without a minder to check her every move.

He was getting soaked. There was a

waterfall sloshing down his spine and making his boxers go soggy.

'*Awwww*,' said Juniper. 'The rain'll wash all the scent messages away.'

'Never mind that! I'm wet through!'

'Come on,' she yelled, through the hissing rain. 'You can shelter in my house until it stops.'

# Chapter Three

U p on the top floor of 19 Canal Street, Juniper's mum was working in her study. She was tapping away on her computer. She had studied the human olfactory organs at Oxford University. She knew all there was to know about noses.

She was writing a kids' book called *The Wonderful World of Smells*. It was her mission to educate modern children. To show them that *all* smells are really exciting.

'Kids! Have you any idea what's up your nose?' she wrote feverishly. 'Yes! There are five million scent cells up there. All for you to smell with! Yet you only use a few of them.'

She stopped typing to wait for some more ideas.

A big green leaf flopped over her shoulder.

Without thinking, she brushed it off. It belonged to a giant plant that took up half her study. It was called a titan arum.

Conditions in the old factory were perfect for it. The ceilings were high, the floors reinforced. The long, tall windows let in loads of sunlight. The titan arum had grown big and jungly. And now it had produced a single flower bud, the size of a small melon.

Back in Victorian times, they'd had a titan arum in Kew Gardens. When the bud burst open, several ladies fainted clean away. Some people called it 'the foulest stench in the world'.

Juniper's mum could hardly wait.

She'd thought enough. She started bashing away on the keys.

'Cast your minds back, kids! Back beyond your ape-man ancestors, to when you were primitive, fishy things swimming in swamps. Then you *really* used those scent cells. You had the same smelling power as a shark. And it can sniff blood from two miles away! But things took a nosedive when you crawled out of the swamp. And it was a total disaster when you stood up on two legs. A nose up in the air is no use! It needs to be close to the ground. So you can snuffle up the most interesting smells like dogs do –'

Juniper's mum took a quick glug of coffee. There was a photo on her desk. You couldn't see a face. Only white teeth and snow goggles and a fur hood, crusted with glittering icicles. It was Juniper's dad. He was a famous Arctic explorer. But he'd fallen into a crevasse two months before Juniper was born. The ice had split open right beneath him; he didn't stand a chance. No trace of him was ever found, except for a single fur-lined mitten.

The old factory was so vast that Juniper's mum didn't hear the door opening six floors down and Kit and her daughter creeping in like drowned rats.

'*Shhh!*' warned Juniper. 'My mum's working upstairs.'

She didn't want her mum to come down. Mum wouldn't approve of other kids in the house. 'They'll fill your head with wrong ideas about smells,' Mum had warned her. 'It's not their fault. They've been brainwashed.'

'Sorry, Mum,' whispered Juniper, inside her

head. 'But I've got to find some friends. Even brainwashed ones.'

'This way,' she told Kit, hustling him through a door.

'Wow,' said Kit, squelching around in his soggy trainers. 'You could fit our whole house in here.'

It was like being inside a cathedral. There was a fridge, a cooker and a washing machine dotted about. But in this huge, airy space they seemed tiny and faraway, like dolls'-house furniture.

Kit wrinkled his nose. What was that stink? It made his eyes water. '*Phew*, can you smell anything?' he asked before he could stop himself. He sniffed again. 'Is that *rotting fish*?'

If anyone had said his house smelled of rotten fish, his mum would have had a fit. She would have blitzed it with a can of air freshener.

But Juniper said proudly, 'Right first time! This place was a cat-food factory before we bought it. Mum says we got a real bargain. They were giving it away.'

'I'm not surprised!'

Juniper wrung out a few of her green

tentacles. 'Mum says the cat-food smell adds character.'

'It's disgusting. *Yurrgh!* Everyone knows that.'

'No, it isn't. You're smell prejudiced.'

'I'm not! I like lots of smells.'

'Except the ones you've been *told* not to. You should think for yourself!'

'What, like you do? You're always saying, my mum said this, my mum said that! Haven't you got a mind of your own?'

They glared at each other. Juniper thought, We just fell out. And we aren't even friends yet.

Was making friends always this tricky?

Kit stared out of the long windows. The rain was just a thin, grey haze. Through it he could see a pale-lemon fuzz ball, struggling to shine.

He said, 'Look, the sun's coming out. I'd better be going.'

Up in Juniper's mum's study, rainbows were chasing each other, like fireflies, all over her walls. She didn't notice them. She was too busy banging on about her favourite subject.

'DNA's dead, kids,' she was typing. 'All that dinosaur-cloning stuff – it's so yesterday! *So what's the hot new science?* I hear you cry! It's smell profiles. Yes, each of you, snuggling in sweaty bits of your body, has your own personal collection of smell molecules that's every bit as individual as your DNA. Go on, sniff your own armpit! Then rush out and tell your friends, "Personal smell profiles are cool!"'

If only all children were like my Juniper, Juniper's mum thought, sighing. She'd raised her daughter to have smell freedom. *Her* sense of smell was completely unspoiled. If only other children knew what they were missing. Sniffing trees and other people's armpits could change their lives!

'Kids! There's a whole new world waiting up your nose,' typed Juniper's mum, in a frenzy of enthusiasm. 'Why don't you explore it, right now?'

Behind her, the fat flower bud of the titan arum swelled another few centimetres.

Juniper's mum took a quick swig of coffee. '*Whoops!*'

She'd absent-mindedly put her mug down

on her single most precious possession. It wasn't the titan arum. That came second on her list. This one sat on her desk. It was a battered old wooden box, about the size of a microwave. It had been made for Dr Thomas Fell way back in Elizabethan times. Screwed to the top of it was an engraved silver plate. It said, 'Dr Thomas Fell – His Cabinet of Human Smells'.

Juniper's mum smiled at the box. She had big plans for Dr Fell's smell collection. It had been a lucky day when she'd come across it in that car boot sale.

After she'd bought the box, she'd done some research. She'd found out all about Dr Fell and his peculiar methods of preserving people's smells. She felt she knew him personally. He hadn't been a very nice bloke. He'd been mixed up in some very dodgy dealings. They even said he dabbled in magic. But Juniper's mum didn't mind that. It just added spice to his story.

'You were a man after my own heart, Dr Thomas Fell,' she said, patting the box.

Like her, he'd believed in the power of smells. As well as being a Master of Smells, he was a Master Swordsman too. You don't often get that combination.

Downstairs, Kit insisted, 'Right. I'm off now. Bye.'

He kept his elbows tightly tucked in as he crossed the kitchen. He didn't want Juniper trying that New Guinea farewell thing again.

But he hesitated by the door. He'd run out of Gladiator. That made him feel really insecure. There were enemies out there, prowling like wolves. He could already hear their sneery voices, 'Here comes Mr Stinky!'

'Don't be so pathetic!' Kit scolded himself. 'You've got to go out there *sometime*.'

Still he didn't leave. The old factory was a freaky place, but at least he didn't feel like an outcast. Where else could you smell like a skunk and be even *more* popular? Where else would someone say, 'Be Proud of Your Armpits'?

Juniper saw him dithering. She thought, Say something interesting.

But the only fascinating facts she knew were about smells.

'Do you know,' she said, 'that they've done

an experiment? They made this class of kids all wear white T-shirts. Then, at home time, the kids took them off, and their mums sniffed the T-shirts. And the mums could tell, just by smelling, which one their own kid had been wearing.'

'Yeah?' said Kit. 'Well, I always thought mums were weird.'

*Brrring, brrring!* Someone was ringing the door bell. Juniper nearly jumped out of her skin. It rang again.

Kit said, 'Aren't you going to let them in?'

Juniper said nervously, 'No one ever comes here.' She and her mum lived a quiet life. Hardly anyone knew that 19 Canal Street existed.

She moved slowly to the door. She opened it. She peeked outside.

'Who is it?' asked Kit.

'They've gone,' said Juniper. 'They left a parcel.'

She came in carrying a white box. GLOBAL SCIENTIFIC SERVICES was stamped on the outside in big, red letters. She put the box on the kitchen table. They both stared at it in dead silence.

'Aren't you going to open it?' asked Kit.

'I already know what it is,' said Juniper. Her voice seemed shaky. Kit couldn't tell whether it was excitement or fear. 'Mum bought it on the Internet – for her smell research. It's an E-Nose.'

'A what?' said Kit.

'That's short for Electronic Nose. It's a new scientific discovery. Mum says it'll change the world of smells forever.'

# Chapter Four

Someone clattered down the stairs shouting, 'Juniper!'

'Quick!' said Juniper. 'Get under the table. It's Mum!'

Kit dived out of sight. The kitchen door creaked open. He felt himself trembling. This mum must be some kind of monster!

'How about nipping out for a hot chocolate with whipped cream and sprinkles?' the monster said. 'Put your coat on. I need a break.'

'Think I'll just stay here,' said Juniper.

'You sure?' Juniper's mum sounded really surprised. 'I'll see you then. I've got some shopping to do.'

Hidden under the table, Kit saw purple biker boots and the hem of a long swishing skirt. It was electric blue, with sparkly gold fringes. Then, like a multicoloured whirlwind, Juniper's mum was gone.

'I won't be long,' she shouted back. A door clashed shut.

Kit crawled out. He felt a mean mood coming on. He didn't like having to cower under tables. It wasn't good for his self-respect. And that had taken a big hammering lately.

'I should have brought my shades,' said Kit. 'Your mum sure likes bright clothes.'

'I do too,' said Juniper smoothing down her lime-green frock. 'Mum says we should celebrate colour. We should use *all* our senses better. But smell is the one we've *most* forgotten about, Mum says.'

'*Mum says, Mum says*,' Kit mocked under his breath. He was sick of hearing what Mum says.

And this Juniper kid thinks *I've* been brainwashed!

Suddenly – he couldn't help it, he'd been good all this time – a streak of spite flicked out, like the tongue of a rattlesnake.

'So what's your dad wearing today? A clown costume?'

'My dad's dead,' said Juniper.

'Oh no, oh no,' howled a voice inside Kit's head. 'Nightmare! Look what you've gone and done now!'

He felt his whole body shrivel up, like a slug drenched with salt.

'Sorry, sorry,' he stammered, blushing bright red. 'I shouldn't have said that. I didn't mean it.'

Juniper gave a stiff little shrug, ''S all right. He was an Arctic explorer. He died ages ago. I never even met him.'

She didn't tell Kit, but she did have something to remember him by. It was better than photos. It was her dad's personal smell profile. It was in the pocket of her party frock at this very moment.

Juniper reached into her pocket. She stroked the furry scrap of material. Her dad's smell molecules were all over it. It came from the lining of his polar mitten – the one that was found beside the crevasse. She carried it everywhere with her, like a comfort blanket.

But even her highly trained nose couldn't pick up his personal smell. Over the years that had faded away completely.

'I'm going to go to the Arctic one day,' whispered Juniper. 'No one will think I'm weird there.'

'Pardon?' said Kit.

But Juniper didn't repeat what she'd said. She just looked really upset.

'You and your big mouth!' Kit told himself, savagely. He whacked the palm of his hand off his forehead. 'Gran warned you about it, didn't she?'

'You going to open that E-Nose?' he gabbled, desperate to change the subject.

'I shouldn't really,' said Juniper. 'Not without Mum here.'

But, secretly, she couldn't wait to get the E-Nose up and running. So she snipped the parcel tape with scissors, then opened the box.

There was a lot of packing. Juniper plunged her arms into the white foam beads.

'Hurry up,' said Kit. He wanted to see what it looked like. The E-Nose sounded strange, a bit sinister. Like everything else in this creepy place.

'Is that it?' said Kit, when Juniper lifted it out. He felt really let down. It was just a

boring, grey, metal box, about the size of a
toaster.

'Why isn't it nose-shaped?'

'Why should it be?' said Juniper. 'It's not like a *human* nose, Mum says. It's just a machine. You put a smell in here.' She slid back a tiny door in the E-Nose. 'And it sort of sniffs it, electronically. It tells you exactly what smell molecules it's made of, then it gives you the recipe. It prints it out, on a piece of paper.'

'Big deal,' said Kit, disappointed. He almost said, 'Big yawn!' But he didn't want to sound sneery. Not after he'd put his foot in it so badly about her dad.

'It's simple really,' said Juniper. 'A child can work it. It's not high-tech or anything. It even runs on batteries.'

'But what *use* is it?' frowned Kit.

'Loads of use! You can rescue lost smells, for a start. Say you've got this old smell that's faded away so a human nose can't smell it. Just stick it in this machine. As long as the *smell molecules* are still there, the E-Nose'll give you the recipe. Then you can make the smell again, good as new!'

'Oh, I get it,' said Kit, at the same time as

he was thinking, Why would you want to do that?

'Look,' he said, 'I'd better go home now.' All this scientific stuff was giving him brain ache.

There were wolves out there waiting. But he'd be ready for them. He took out his Gladiator, to give his armpits a few quick squirts.

He shook it. '*Awwww*, no!' He'd forgotten it was empty.

'Hey,' said Juniper, staring at the can. 'You know what we were wondering before – what a Roman gladiator *really* smells like?'

'What's that got to do with anything!' roared Kit. 'The main thing is, I've got no deodorant! How am I going to survive out there on the streets?'

Juniper obviously didn't appreciate his problem. She was about as streetwise as a newborn baby. She didn't even *try* to help him out. Instead she said, 'Because, now the E-Nose has arrived, we can find out.'

'What?' Kit was so startled he stopped panicking about his personal smell. 'You're kidding me!'

But she'd already grabbed the E-Nose.

'Come on,' she said.

Kit followed her into the factory. It seemed to him like a grim place to grow up. You wouldn't call it cosy. There were no carpets or wallpaper. Just rough bare bricks and cold metal stairs.

'Where're we going?' he asked, clanging up the iron stairs after her.

'To Mum's study,' she called back. 'That's where she keeps Dr Fell's Cabinet of Human Smells.'

# Chapter Five

'**W**ow!' said Kit. 'It's a jungle in here! What's that monster plant?'

'It's a titan arum,' Juniper told him. 'Ladies faint when it opens.'

'Ex*cuse* me?'

But Juniper didn't want to talk about the world's smelliest plant. It was the E-Nose that excited her. She put it down on Mum's desk.

She dragged Dr Fell's Cabinet of Human Smells towards her.

'This box is from Elizabethan times,' she told Kit.

It had two trays in the front that slid out. She pulled out the bottom one.

'*Aaaaargh!*' said Kit, his eyes bulging.

'Whoops, sorry, wrong one,' said Juniper, sliding it back.

Kit pointed a trembling finger. 'I saw – I saw,' he stammered.

'Oh, it's nothing to worry about,' said Juniper briskly. 'It's just Dr Fell's collection of false noses.'

She pulled out the tray again. There, nestling in red velvet, were three false noses – one wooden, one silver, one gold.

'There's a glue pot,' said Juniper, picking up a small silver pot with a hinged lid. 'He took one everywhere with him. But none of that is important. It's his *smell* collection that's really interesting.'

She started to slide the tray back in.

'Wait, wait,' pleaded Kit. 'I've got to know! Who was this Elizabethan guy? Why did he need these false noses?'

'Because his own was sliced off in a sword fight. The wooden one was for every day and the posh gold one was for parties. Dr Fell was a bit peculiar. But I'll tell you about him later.'

She was already sliding out the top tray. Kit saw rows of glass vials, each plugged with red wax. Most were cracked and broken. Whatever was in them had leaked out, but four were still filled with oily, amber fluid.

Juniper picked one of those up, very carefully.

'This is the Gladiator's smell,' she said. 'Preserved in Dr Fell's special oil.'

She squinted at a little label. Back in Elizabethan times, Dr Fell had stuck on that label, with glue from his tiny pot. The same glue he used to fix on his false noses.

'The writing's hard to read,' said Juniper screwing up her eyes. 'It says *Essence of Gladiator*. *Essence* is an old-fashioned word for smell.'

Sun slanted through the long windows. It hit the vial. The Essence of Gladiator glowed, like fiery gold. Juniper shook the vial. There was something inside the oil. Brown, stringy bits of something.

'That's probably a piece of the Gladiator's clothes,' she said. 'It would work best if it was a sweaty piece, Mum says. You know, soaked with his smell molecules.'

Juniper didn't know it, but it was a few fibres from a gladiator's jockstrap. His jockstrap had been on his skeleton, inside his stone coffin, under some Roman ruins. But that didn't stop Dr Fell from stealing it.

It wasn't the first time he'd been grave robbing.

Kit tried to sort out his jumbled brain. 'Have I got this right? This Dr Fell guy saved people's smells? By bunging bits of their sweaty clothes in some special oil? That's sick!'

'It's science! Course, he didn't *know* about smell molecules. He just knew a person's smell was a really important part of them.'

'I still think it's sick,' murmured Kit. But he couldn't help asking, 'So what's this Gladiator smell like?'

'I don't know,' said Juniper. 'We've never opened the vial.'

'Never opened it!' said Kit, amazed. 'Weren't you even curious?'

'Course,' said Juniper. 'But we were scared we'd spill it or something. Then it would be lost forever. But now we've got the E-Nose, we don't have to worry about that.'

'I get it!' said Kit. At last something made sense. 'You put the Gladiator smell in the E-Nose and it tells you the recipe. And then you can make it again.'

'We could make buckets of it if we wanted to,' said Juniper.

But she was still dithering. Why didn't she open the vial?

'Mum should be here,' she said.

'Forget about your mum,' said Kit, impatiently.

Juniper took a deep breath.

'Go on, I dare you,' said Kit.

Juniper pulled out the wax plug.

'Let me smell it first,' said Kit.

He put his nose near. What would a *real* gladiator smell like? He'd seen films. He'd read about what went on in Roman arenas. It was all coming alive in his head. The mob baying for blood, the slaughter, the fear. He braced himself for a whiff of sawdust soaked with gore and the dung of terrified wild animals.

'Here we go!' Kit wrinkled his nose. He sucked in a great, big hooterful.

Then let out an outraged roar. 'I can't smell anything! Nothing at all!'

He felt really cheated. Juniper *must* be making fun of him! After Laura and Sophie, he felt very sensitive about that. Was this whole Dr Fell thing some kind of set-up? Was Juniper even in league with Laura and her friends?

He whirled round, half expecting Laura to come out from behind the titan arum, smirking: 'See, he smells. And he's stupid as well.'

He was furious with himself. He'd really been taken in. He'd believed all that smell stuff she'd told him. He'd trusted her! She was the strangest kid he'd ever met. But she didn't seem like a liar.

'I can't smell a gladiator!' he insisted angrily.

Juniper didn't seem surprised. 'Course you can't,' she said, coolly taking the vial back. 'That smell's two thousand years old. A dog couldn't even sniff him.'

'Oh, right.' Kit calmed down. Perhaps she wasn't trying to trick him after all. 'But you can smell scent messages on trees,' he said. 'Can't you smell anything?'

Juniper took a deep sniff herself. 'Nope,' she said, shaking her head. 'But maybe his smell molecules are still there. That's what matters.' She switched on the E-Nose. 'Let's find out.'

Nothing happened. The ON light didn't glow green. They waited.

Behind them, stealthily, the titan arum bud swelled just a millimetre more.

'That E-Nose is rubbish!' said Kit. 'It's broke! Typical! Never buy *anything* off the Internet. That's what my dad says.'

'Stupid! You forgot about the batteries,' Juniper scolded herself.

She found some in her mum's desk drawer and slotted them in. 'Try again,' she murmured.

This time the little grey box came to life. It whirred. Tiny lights started twinkling.

'It's working!' said Juniper. She sounded thrilled. But still she hesitated. Should she go ahead without Mum? She and Mum were like best friends. In fact, until this morning, Mum was her *only* friend.

Juniper stroked the tiny piece of Dad's mitten. She'd made up her mind.

'I'm going to put some Gladiator essence in the E-Nose,' she told Kit. 'Once we've got the recipe, they can make it up in a laboratory. Then you'll *really* be able to smell him.'

'A lab?' said Kit. 'You never said anything about a lab.'

'You didn't think we could make it here, did you?' said Juniper.

Kit felt flat and disappointed. He'd got himself all excited. He wanted to smell that gladiator NOW.

'So how long will making it in a lab take?' he asked. But, somehow, he wasn't that interested any more.

Juniper shrugged. 'Dunno. Could be days, weeks, Mum says. Maybe months to get it exactly right.'

Kit sighed. 'I might as well go home then,' he said.

But Juniper wasn't listening. She couldn't wait to test the E-Nose. Because, if it worked with the Gladiator, then maybe she could rescue her dad's lost smell. And keep his essence with her, always.

She opened the sliding door in the machine. She tipped in some of Dr Fell's Essence of Gladiator. Only a few drops of golden oil and some jockstrap fibres. Just enough for the E-Nose to break down and analyse.

'Hope that's enough,' she said. She put the wax plug back in the vial. 'I don't know *exactly* how this E-Nose thing works.'

'Maybe you *should* wait until your mum comes home,' said Kit, feeling suddenly nervous. He felt guilty now for daring her to do it. 'What if it goes wrong?'

They waited again. Nothing seemed to be happening. Kit wandered over to a window.

Suddenly Juniper cried out, 'Look, it's doing its stuff! It's printing out the smell molecules!'

Kit came rushing back. The E-Nose was whirring away. A ribbon of white tape jerked out the top, with nail-biting slowness. Kit watched it for a few seconds. Was that *all* it did? He'd thought it would do something spectacular!

He peered at the tape coming out. 'That's *gladiator* smell?'

It was some kind of graph, just a load of squiggly lines. 'I can't make any sense of it.'

'Yes, but scientists can. Mum's going to get loads and loads of Essence of Gladiator made up in a laboratory.'

Kit tried not to sound sneery. 'What for, exactly?'

'She's got this great idea. She's going to make a scratch-and-sniff book for children. Just put some Essence of Gladiator on the page –'

'It's been done,' Kit butted in.

It was obvious Juniper and her mum didn't get out much. He'd seen loads of kids' history books that said, 'Scratch here to smell a medieval midden.' Or, 'Scratch here to smell a mouldy old mummy.'

'But this is different,' Juniper insisted. 'My mum's will say, "Scratch here to smell a *real* person from the past –"'

She stopped abruptly. 'What's wrong with the E-Nose?'

It was chattering like an angry squirrel. The chattering rose to a buzz-saw whine, then a terrible, ear-splitting wail.

Kit covered his ears. 'Stop it! It's going berserk!'

Its lights were flashing on and off. It was spewing out white tape like a supermarket till gone mad!

'What's wrong with it?' yelled Juniper. Then, suddenly, she threw her head back like a dog and sniffed the air.

'What's that smell?' she said.

Even Kit could smell it. You didn't need a highly trained nose. It wasn't the titan arum – its bud hadn't burst yet. Besides, this smell was quite pleasant.

From somewhere in the study came great gusts of flowery scent.

'I'm getting jasmine,' said Juniper, 'and lavender and roses – and geraniums.'

'*Phew!* It's like old ladies' perfume!' said Kit, crinkling his nose in disgust.

'But it's greasy,' said Juniper, frowning. 'And, what's this? I'm getting a whiff of pigeon dung.'

'Pigeon dung?' said Kit.

'It's what they dyed their hair with.'

'Who did?' begged Kit, his mind boggling. '*Who* dyed their hair?' He'd totally lost the plot. 'What are you *talking* about?'

'Gladiators,' said Juniper. 'They dyed their hair blond with pigeon dung. Mum says.'

She stared at the E-Nose. It had quietened down now. It had stopped spewing out coils of white tape. It seemed to have finished its job.

Even Juniper couldn't understand it. 'It can't *make* these old smells,' she said, puzzled. 'I'm sure it can't. It only works out what smell molecules are in them –'

'You're saying,' Kit butted in, 'that gladiators smelled like that!' All his illusions were shattered. 'I thought they were big, tough, hairy blokes! And *you're* telling me they were sissies who smelled of geraniums!'

'Mum says they rubbed on scented oils,' said Juniper, impatiently, 'before they went out to fight. But that's not the point! Don't you get it? *This E-Nose isn't supposed to make smells.*'

'Maybe it's some kind of new, improved model,' said Kit.

'*Ouch!*' came a gruff grunt, from behind the titan arum.

Juniper's head whipped round. 'Who said that? That's not Mum's voice.'

She dived in among the big leaves. Five seconds later, she backed out again. Her face had gone deathly pale.

'What's the matter?' asked Kit, anxiously. 'You all right?' For some reason, he was shivering too. The hairs on the back of his neck were wriggling like worms.

When Juniper spoke, her voice was a small, scared whisper.

'You know I thought the E-Nose couldn't make smells? Well, it can do more than that. It can make people.'

# Chapter Six

'*O*uch!' came the deep, gruff voice again, from among the titan arum leaves.

'You mean, that's *him*? The actual Gladiator from Roman times?' gasped Kit. 'This can't be happening.'

Juniper seemed in a daze. She was still staring at the E-Nose. 'I don't understand it.' It was only supposed to break down and analyse smell molecules. Not assemble them again into people!'

'Never mind that now,' hissed Kit. 'What's he doing back there?'

'*Ouch!*'

'Why's he making that noise?'

Juniper shook herself. She tried to concentrate on Kit's questions. 'Er, I think he's in pain,' she said.

Kit knew a bit about gladiators. Maybe this  guy had been in a duel to the death in a Roman arena – with a gladiator who fought with a net and trident!

'Is he wounded?' whispered Kit. If he was, Kit could forgive him for wearing old ladies' perfume. Perhaps.

'No, he doesn't look like he's wounded.'

'But you said he was in pain.'

'He is. He's pulling out his chest hair with a pair of tweezers.'

'You're making this up.'

Kit barged through the jungly titan arum leaves. He was sure she was playing some kind of stupid game. What can you expect from girls who go around sniffing trees?

But that flowery scent was really strong now. It made his eyes water.

He ducked under the last leaf.

*She's telling the truth.*

He suddenly felt hot and dizzy. His brain was in tangles, trying to cope. He screwed his eyes tightly shut and told himself, 'This can't be happening. Right?'

When he opened them again, the Gladiator was still there. He was sitting with his back against the wall, wearing what looked like leather bikini bottoms. His hair was bleached blond with pigeon dung. His body was greasy and glistening with sweet-smelling oils.

'*Ouch.*' He plucked out another chest hair.

The Gladiator spent a lot of time making himself look drop-dead gorgeous. But it was all worth it. He drove the Roman ladies wild. They didn't like nasty, hairy brutes. They liked their gladiators smooth and smelling nice, with the latest hairstyles.

'Tut, tut, tut,' he clucked fussily. He'd forgotten to clean out his earwax.

His ear scoop was on a bronze ring with his tweezers and nail file and a little round mirror. He kept his beauty aids handy at all times, hanging from his belt. A gladiator always has to look his best. He had his sword and shield lying across his knees. He kept them handy at all times too.

Kit couldn't believe it. Not that the E-Nose could make people from smell molecules – he had the evidence right before his eyes – but that gladiators weren't at all like he expected.

'He's really vain,' Kit murmured. Like a  film star. The Gladiator was squinting into the mirror, checking his hairstyle.

'Oh no. He's filing his nails now.'

'He doesn't look all that bright,' said Juniper, suddenly creeping up beside Kit.

'*Shhh*, he'll hear you.'

The Gladiator grunted, '*Doh?*'

He was a Roman lady's dream. And a mean killing machine. But Juniper was right. He was as thick as a brick.

His low forehead scrunched up. His tiny eyes looked puzzled. Had he heard something? There was a message going from his ears to his brain. It was just taking an awfully long time to get there.

Finally, he put down his nail file and grabbed his shield and sword: '*Grrrr!*'

He wasn't a sophisticated fighter. His speciality was hacking his opponent to bits, without messing up his hair. He looked around, scowling.

'Run!' said Kit.

But they didn't need to. As the Gladiator lumbered to his feet, he suddenly dissolved, into millions of tiny stars.

Kit's mouth dropped open. His dazzled eyes seemed big as moons. 'What are those?'

'They're smell molecules. We can see them!'

They whizzed about in a swarm, like glittering fireflies, then shot off in all directions and fizzled out. Only a flowery fragrance still hung in the air.

Kit gazed at the place where the Gladiator had just been. He was shaken to the core. For starters, because he'd just seen a *real* gladiator. And, for seconds, because, *before* he saw him, those guys had been his heroes.

'I thought they spent all their spare time practising combat skills,' he murmured to himself in disgust. Not making themselves smell lovely. Not plucking their chests, dyeing their hair with pigeon dung and admiring themselves in mirrors.

He felt really cheated. Those films he'd seen, those books he'd read – they were all wrong!

He pulled his can of Gladiator out of his pocket. After this, he was *definitely* going to buy a different deodorant.

'No one would buy this stuff at all,' he decided, 'if they knew what gladiators were *really* like.'

He marched over to a window, pushed it up  and hurled the small silver can into the canal.

The black rat saw it coming. He couldn't believe his luck. Help had arrived from the heavens! His burger box had gone all soggy and was seconds from sinking. With a daring leap, he abandoned ship. Clinging to the deodorant can, he reached the safety of the canal bank at last.

For a few moments Kit felt panicky. Why had he chucked the can out of the window? Without Gladiator in his pocket, he felt unprotected.

Then he remembered. It was empty. And, anyway, he didn't need it here at 19 Canal Street where if someone said, 'You smell!' you replied, 'Thanks very much!'

Where was Juniper by the way? She'd gone very quiet. He turned away from the window. She was standing by the E-Nose, fitting in some more batteries. After what had just happened, she seemed strangely cool. As if she saw gladiators assembled from their smell molecules every day.

'What are you doing?' asked Kit.

'It needs new ones already,' she said. She

seemed to be talking to herself, as if Kit wasn't in the room. 'Making the Gladiator used up all their power. I think that's why he broke up like that – cos the batteries ran out.'

'You're not making him again are you?' asked Kit. There was still some of Dr Fell's Essence of Gladiator left in the vial. 'I just want to forget all about him.'

'I'm not interested in him either,' said Juniper.

Suddenly Kit was scared by the look on her face. She seemed desperate, but deter-mined. There was a kind of wild hope in her eyes.

'I just need two more batteries,' she said, hunting in the desk drawers. 'Here're some!' She twirled round. The frills from her princess frock swept the Gladiator vial off the desk.

There was a tinkling sound.

'Look what you've done now!' said Kit horrified. He crouched down to inspect the damage. The glass vial was cracked. The oil was leaking out in a golden puddle. 'What's your mum going to say?'

But Juniper hadn't even noticed. She had other things on her mind.

She took a tatty fragment of fur out of her  pocket.

'What's that?' asked Kit.

'It's the lining of my dad's polar mitten.'

Oh no, thought Kit. Not that dead dad again.

He'd already upset her once. He just wished she'd keep off the subject. I don't want to know any more details, he thought.

But Juniper was telling him things, in a rush of words. 'He was an Arctic explorer, really brave. Look, there's his photo.'

Kit took a quick sideways glance. He saw a fur-fringed hood, snow goggles, a beard spiky with snow crystals.

'He was sledging to the North Pole,' said Juniper, 'when this crevasse opened up, right under his feet. All they found was this mitten –'

'Wait a minute!' Kit knew he shouldn't interrupt when she was telling him such a tragic tale. But he couldn't help it. He'd just had a grotesque thought. It was growing, like a monster, in his brain.

'Does this mitten thing, by any chance, have your dad's *smell molecules* on it?'

He hoped she'd say, 'No! What a dumb idea!' But instead she said, eagerly, 'How did you guess?'

Her whole plan suddenly lit up Kit's brain in one sickening flash.

'No!' he cried. 'You're not going to assemble your dad?'

He looked round desperately. Where was her mum?

I need help! he thought. I can't handle this!

It wasn't the time for smart remarks. But without them he felt tongue-tied.

Juniper was frantic to get going. She sounded really happy. Words gushed out of her mouth so fast he could hardly follow. 'I couldn't wait for this E-Nose to come. I thought, I'll be able to make Essence of Dad. But I never dreamed I'd be able to make *him*.'

Kit's skin was crawling. His brain shrieked at him, 'This is a nightmare! This is all wrong! *Say something*!'

Words popped out of his mouth. 'It's going to cost you a fortune in batteries.'

Was that a cruel, heartless thing to say? He couldn't tell any more. He was too mixed up.

'Cos he'll break up, won't he?' Then Kit added quickly, 'Just like the Gladiator did. Unless you keep putting new batteries in all the time.'

Juniper wasn't listening anyway. She had the mitten lining in her hand. She was tugging off a tiny tuft of fur and feeding it into the E-Nose.

Kit warned himself, 'Keep your mouth shut.' Gran was right. It just got him into trouble.

Juniper switched on the E-Nose. The little light glowed green. Slowly, slowly, the white tape jerked out, scribbled with blue squiggly lines.

It's starting, thought Kit. This is like something out of a horror movie!

Only it wasn't the movies. This was real life. You only had to see that look of longing on Juniper's face. That wasn't pretend.

Kit could hardly breathe. A feeling of dread suffocated him. It scuttled all over him, like ants. Was there a chill in the room? Or was it just his own fear?

His eyes darted here, there. Where would Juniper's Arctic-explorer dad appear? Maybe his smell would come first. What does an Arctic explorer smell like?

But why wasn't the E-Nose making that terrible racket? Why hadn't the tape speeded up?

'It's not working!' cried Juniper.

Kit came to look. The E-Nose had gone back to humming quietly. It had finished the job.

'There's Dad's smell recipe there. But that's all,' said Juniper. Her voice was trembly with tears.

Kit felt really awkward. He didn't know how to comfort her. 'At least you got the recipe,' he said.

Juniper smeared the hot tears all over her face. 'I was stupid to think it would make my dad.'

'Maybe it only works with stuff out of Dr Fell's smell cabinet,' said Kit. 'Maybe that oil's got something to do with it.' He didn't have a clue what he was talking about really. He was just grabbing ideas out of thin air.

'That must be it,' Juniper surprised him by answering. She shook herself, as if she was shaking herself free from a dream.

'I should have thought of that,' she said. 'And you're right, at least I got his smell recipe.'

That was all she'd expected in the first place. She ripped off the bit of tape with her dad's personal smell profile on it. She folded it up and put it in the pocket of her party frock.

Kit looked at her gratefully. So he hadn't been cruel. He *could* say things that made people feel better.

Then Juniper said a strange thing. She'd stopped crying. But her voice still seemed very tiny and far away.

'There are no smells in the Arctic,' she told Kit.

'Pardon?' said Kit. At first he thought he'd heard wrong. Then he said, 'Are you sure?'

Her voice got stronger. 'You ever tried sniffing an ice cube? When the smell molecules are frozen up, you can't smell anything. I'm going to go and live in the Arctic, when I'm old enough.'

'It'd be dead boring,' said Kit. 'Nothing but ice and snow. For miles and miles.'

'It wouldn't,' said Juniper. 'And no one

could make fun of me for smelling the wrong things. Cos no one can smell anything there anyway.'

There were loads of books in the house about the North Pole that had belonged to her dad. She often looked at the pictures. Imagined herself in that smell-less world, among frozen snow fields and glittering icebergs.

Would she be happy there? What choice did she have? 'I'll never fit in here,' said Juniper sadly. 'I'll never have any friends.'

Kit was shocked. He thought she was quite happy being a tree-sniffing freak! He hadn't realized she felt so lonely and left out.

'No!' he startled her by shouting. 'You *won't* have to go to the North Pole! You *will* fit in with other kids. Trust me! It won't be that tough. You'll just have to learn about nice and nasty smells. Armpits for instance –'

A door clashed downstairs.

'It's Mum!' said Juniper. 'She's back!'

# Chapter Seven

J uniper said, in an urgent voice, 'Get the E-Nose.'

'Aren't you going to tell your mum about the Gladiator?' asked Kit, grabbing the machine.

If you sniffed hard, you could still smell his flowery fragrance in the air. But his essence was leaking out of the cracked vial and soaking into the carpet.

'And all the other stuff?' Kit added.

He didn't *specifically* mention trying to remake her dad from a piece of furry mitten. That topic was a minefield. He didn't want to upset her again.

Juniper didn't answer anyway. She was sliding out a tray from Dr Fell's Cabinet of Human Smells. '*Whoops*, wrong one, I always do that.'

It was Dr Fell's collection – a nose for every occasion. This time, besides his glue pot and three false noses, Kit saw something else. It was nestling in red velvet, beside the party nose. It was nose-sized. But horribly wrinkled and black.

*Yuk!* What's that? he thought. But did he really want to know? Besides, Juniper had already pushed the tray back in.

She opened the top tray and grabbed the three unbroken vials. She only wanted one. But she didn't have time to decipher the tiny writing. So she took them all. She stashed them in the pocket of her frock.

'Let's go,' she said to Kit. 'Before Mum gets here. Hang on . . .'

Gingerly, she picked up the broken vial from the floor. She didn't want Mum to find it. There was about a teaspoonful of Essence of Gladiator left in the bottom, but that would soon leak away.

Together, they sneaked out of the door of the study. Kit didn't mind running. He didn't want to meet Juniper's mum. He was sure she would give him a hard time about his smell prejudice. 'Do you believe in the power of smells? Do you sniff trees? Well, why not?'

Juniper's mum came clattering up the iron stairs. Her biker boots made every step ring like gongs.

Kit looked down the stairwell. He saw a head coming up. Its hair was spiky and dyed bright purple. Little lights twinkled around its eyebrows.

'Hey,' hissed Kit, 'your mum's got diamond eyebrow studs!'

But Juniper hissed back, 'She'll see you. Come on, down the back way.'

While Kit and Juniper crept downstairs, Juniper's mum settled herself at her desk. She was refreshed after her break and raring to go. She switched on her computer. While it was revving up, she spun round in her chair to check the titan arum.

Not long now, she thought. That flower bud was bigger than a green rugby ball.

She spun back to her desk. She wanted to finish *The Wonderful World of Smells* before the E-Nose arrived. Because, after that, she would be busy with her really big project, *Find Out What People From the Past Really Smelled Like*. It wasn't the snappiest book title. But Juniper's mum wasn't going to waste time thinking up wacky titles. She wanted children to take her books *seriously*.

But all that was in the future. For now she must concentrate on Chapter 89 of *The Wonderful World of Smells*. She started tapping feverishly. She wanted to tell children about one of the forgotten figures of the world of smells, Dr Thomas Fell.

'Back in Elizabethan times,' she typed, 'Dr Thomas Fell had everything going for him. He was popular, handsome and rich. He was a respected smell historian, preserving smells for future generations. He was Queen Elizabeth's favourite scent maker, a powerful figure at Court. It's even said he invented Sir Walter Raleigh's strawberry cologne! But then, after he lost his nose in a duel, his fortunes went downhill –'

It's tragic really, thought Juniper's mum, lifting her hands off the keys and staring into space, how quickly it all went wrong.

Dr Fell couldn't appear at Court noseless. Everyone would mock him! And someone as high up as him had many enemies. They were already gathering like wolves. So he started a desperate search to find a new hooter.

He thought he'd cracked it with the gold nose. He glued it on to his face, dressed in his finest clothes and rushed to Court.

'Your servant, Ma'am,' he said, sweeping aside his cape and bowing low to Queen Elizabeth.

*Clink.* The glue gave way. His false nose fell off and hopped across the floor. All the courtiers howled with laughter. Even the Queen was in fits.

Dr Fell was a proud man. He couldn't stand the shame. So he banished himself from the Court and moved to Wales.

His life was in tatters. He'd already been sacked as Queen Elizabeth's scent maker. What good is a scent maker who can't smell?

After that, he vanished from history. Juniper's mum had done loads of research, read piles of Elizabethan documents. But she'd only found one or two mentions of him, here and there. They said he became a bitter and twisted person. Started practising the dark arts, grave robbing. Local people were scared stiff of him. Some said he should have been burned as a warlock.

There was even talk of kidnapping – rumours he'd stolen a child from a travelling fair. But Juniper's mum wasn't going to put that into her children's book. It was far too scary.

And, besides, she thought, it probably isn't true.

While Juniper's mum tapped away at the top of 19 Canal Street, Kit and Juniper were down in the cellar.

Kit put the E-Nose on top of an old barrel. Then stared around. It was even more bleak and grim down here than in the rest of the factory. For a start, there was no daylight. There was only a single bulb, glowing yellow above their heads. Kit could see shadowy corners, alcoves, caves, all built out of bare, red brick. But most of the cellar was in darkness.

And it was so damp and drippy. There was moss everywhere, growing on the floor and walls like big, green sponges. Was that water he could hear trickling? It felt as if the canal was trying to get in. As if it was pressing on the  cellar walls.

Something flopped through the darkness. 'What's that?' said Kit, startled.

'It's only a frog,' said Juniper. 'Lots of frogs and toads live down here. They like it.'

There were urgent things Kit wanted to ask Juniper. Such as, 'Did I *really* see a Roman gladiator?' And, 'Why didn't you tell your mum what happened?'

Instead he said, 'How do you *know* it's a frog? You can't even see it. It might be a toad.'

He'd forgotten her super-sensitive nose. Juniper sniffed again, to make sure. 'I know it's a frog,' she said, 'because it smells froggy. Mmmmm.'

Kit sighed. Was he mad staying here? Then he reminded himself, 'She *likes* the smell of frog. Whatever *you* smell like, it's not going to matter.'

And it was true that, since he'd stepped inside Juniper's house, he'd hardly given a thought to his own armpits. But that might be because there were plenty of other things for him to worry about.

'So why are we down here?' asked Kit, shivering. 'Can't we go back to the kitchen?'

'That reminds me,' said Juniper. She still had the cracked Gladiator vial in her fist. She nipped up to the kitchen and tucked it into the rubbish bin. Under yesterday's cold macaroni cheese.

Some more Essence of Gladiator had dribbled out. She tried scrubbing it off her fingers with a bit of kitchen towel.

When she came dashing back, Kit protested again, 'I'd rather be in the kitchen. This place is like a dungeon.'

'But Mum might come to the kitchen, to make a coffee or something. And I don't want her to see what we're doing.'

'What are we doing?' asked Kit. Dark suspicions were already spreading through his brain. 'And what did you take those vials for?'

Juniper took the three unbroken vials from her pocket. She held one up to the light. The amber oil flashed like flames.

Like the Gladiator vial, they all had brown, stringy bits suspended inside them. And, like his, they'd been carefully labelled by Dr Fell.

'Each one of these vials,' said Juniper, in a  hushed voice, 'has a person inside it.'

Kit's skin was crawling again – that sounded so spooky. And being down here in this tomb-like cellar didn't make things any better.

'Come on,' said Kit, 'you're not going to use the E-Nose again, are you? To make people?'

He hated to bring it up. But he had to mention it. 'It didn't work when you tried making your dad.'

'That's why I've got to use it again,' said Juniper. 'You know what you said before? About it only working because of the *way* Dr Fell preserved the person's smell?'

'I can't remember saying that.'

'Well, you said it was all down to his special oil.'

'I was talking rubbish,' said Kit desperately. 'I talk rubbish all the time.'

'No, I think you were right. If I could find out what was in the oil, I could make some. Then put a bit of my dad's mitten in it . . .'

Oh no, thought Kit. He felt himself squirming inside. She still wanted to assemble her dad from his smell molecules!

He thought she'd given that up.

Kit wanted to shout out, 'I don't want anything to do with bringing back your dead dad!' But he couldn't say something so cruel – not when he was trying his best to be kind. So he just said, 'How can you find out what's in the oil?'

'I'll get Dr Fell to tell me,' said Juniper, as if it was obvious. 'He preserved his own smell molecules in one of these vials.'

'You're kidding me!'

'Look,' said Juniper, holding up a vial in the disc of dim yellow light.

Kit squinted hard at the spidery writing.

*Essence of Myself*, it said on the label.

'That's him,' said Juniper, shaking the vial gently. In the depths of the oil, golden fire seemed to flicker. You could see scraps of material. Were they from Dr Fell's ruff or his lace-trimmed gloves, or his silky stockings?

'But didn't you say he was a bit *peculiar*?' protested Kit.

'That was mainly *after* his false nose fell off in front of the Queen,' Juniper explained. 'And the whole Court mocked him. Mum says it turned him a bit funny. He spent the rest of his life trying to find a new nose. It nearly got him arrested.'

'Why?' asked Kit.

He wasn't sure he wanted to know. He could hear frogs and toads flopping about in dark corners. This cellar was creepy enough, without hearing Dr Fell's story.

'Well, he went grave robbing.' Even Juniper, who could stand the stinkiest smells, looked slightly queasy. 'For new noses.'

'What're you telling me?' gasped Kit. 'Are you telling me he stole dead people's noses? And tried to make them grow on his own face? That's really gross!'

Juniper gave him a sickly grin. 'He thought if a nose grew, it wouldn't keep falling off. And he might even be able to smell through it. Mum says he was ahead of his time. Nose grafts are no problem now. They can grow you a new nose on your own arm. Course, they didn't have the technology then –'

'Don't try to make excuses for him!' Kit butted in. 'The guy's a ghoul!'

Then something else struck him. 'Wait a second! That shrivelled black thing in his nose collection?' Kit thought he was going to throw up. His stomach was twisting itself into knots. 'He didn't get that grave robbing, did he?'

Juniper looked offended. 'Just how weird do you think we are?' she demanded.

'What, on a scale of one to ten?' shouted Kit. 'Ten and a half!'

'Calm down,' said Juniper. 'We wouldn't keep something like that. That's not a human nose – it's a prune from Mum's muesli. Don't know how it ended up in there.'

*Phew*, thought Kit. He felt a bit stupid now, as if he'd got himself all worked up over nothing.

'Well, it *might* have been a nose,' he mumbled. 'Haven't you ever seen Egyptian mummies?' He meant the bits poking out through the bandages. They were black and withered like that.

Juniper switched on the E-Nose.

'You're not going ahead with this, are you?' asked Kit. 'I just don't think reassembling this Dr Fell guy is a good idea.'

Juniper's face was stubborn. 'He'll only be here for a few minutes,' she said. 'Until the batteries run out.'

A few minutes was all she needed to ask him about his secret oil.

Kit lost it again. 'Oh, great! That's just great! That makes it *perfectly* all right then!' He was using his best sneery voice. He couldn't help it – this had gone way beyond being kind.

'You shouldn't be messing about with things like this,' said Kit, shuddering. 'It's sick! It's scary!'

Juniper looked scared too. So why wasn't it stopping her? Kit knew why. It was because she wanted her dad back so badly.

He had to save her from herself. She wasn't thinking straight. 'Give me those vials!' Kit made a grab for them.

'No!' She tried to hide them behind her back, but they slipped out of her fingers, still greasy with gladiator oil.

'They're broken now!' she wailed.

Kit sighed. 'Thank goodness.' He felt desperately sorry for her, but it was the best thing.

Juniper crouched down and fumbled for the vials in the dark.

'They're here!' she shouted joyfully. 'They're

not smashed!' They'd fallen on a cushion of soggy moss.

Kit cursed under his breath. What was he going to do now? 'Get out of here!' his brain told him. It was a brilliant suggestion. But he just couldn't do it.

'I can't read the labels,' said Juniper. 'They've come off.'

That glue Dr Fell used for sticking his noses on had never been much good.

'I don't know which vial is Dr Fell now,' said Juniper in despair.

There was already another question in Kit's mind. It was the first time he'd thought about it. 'Whose smells are in the other two vials?' he asked her.

Juniper didn't hesitate. She knew those labels off by heart. She and her mum had looked at Dr Fell's smell collection so many times.

'One said *Essence of Pig Woman*,' she told Kit. 'And the other said *Essence of Monster*.'

Kit couldn't believe it. Here was a whole set of new horrors. His poor overcrowded brain couldn't cope. 'Did you just say *monster*?'

But the question hardly had time to burst

out of his mouth when Juniper said, 'I'll just have to choose.'

Kit pleaded frantically. 'You can't go ahead with it! I just told you, we're messing with things we don't understand.'

'It's only science,' said Juniper. 'Cloning humans from DNA. Making them from smell molecules. What's the difference?'

'You're kidding me!' said Kit. *If* this was science, it was the spookiest science he'd ever seen.

'If I don't get Dr Fell first time,' Juniper said, 'I'll try again until I do.'

But deep inside her a shaky voice kept saying, 'Shouldn't you stop this now?'

Kit was right, it was all getting out of control.

Yet meeting her dad, even for a few minutes, would make it all worth it. She would take any risks . . .

The E-Nose was waiting, its green light winking away. It looked like such a friendly little machine. It made it all seem so easy.

Juniper slid open the tiny door. She picked one of the vials. She meant to dribble in a few drops of amber oil. But her hand shook and the whole lot tipped in.

She frowned. 'There's none left now. It had better work first time.'

The tape came slithering out. *Please*, let it just give the smell recipe, Kit was thinking. But Dr Fell's oil was working its magic.

'Oh no,' groaned Kit, as the E-Nose went manic.

Who was it making from smell molecules? Pig Woman? Monster? Or Dr Fell? Every nerve in Kit's body tingled. His eyes twitched about, checking the cellar's dark depths.

The E-Nose stopped flashing and shrieking. It had finished assembling.

I bet it's old No-Nose, thought Kit, his eyes searching the shadows. But there was no sign of the sinister Dr Fell. Kit listened, but he couldn't hear a false nose falling off and clinking on to the cellar floor.

'Can you smell it?' asked Juniper.

Great wafts of flowery scent, sweet and sickly.

'It's not that Gladiator come back again, is it?' cried Kit. He listened for the telltale sounds of chest hair being yanked out: '*Ow! Ow!*'

'No, it's not him,' answered Juniper. 'This is

another scent. I think it's *violets*!' She sounded  really surprised.

Violets? thought Kit. It's probably not Pig Woman then.

He wasn't sure what a Pig Woman was, but he guessed she would pong something terrible.

Then he saw what the E-Nose had assembled.

It was lying curled up on the floor like a dormouse. Its tatty head was tucked between its feet. It had a big toe stuffed in each ear. It seemed to be sleeping.

Was it human? Kit went closer and peered at it.

'Phew,' he said. 'I thought for a minute there it was the Monster. But it's only a little boy.'

'I chose the wrong vial,' said Juniper sadly. 'We'll just have to try again.'

The boy twitched in his sleep like a dog. Kit jumped back. Shuddering himself awake, the boy took his toes out of his ears and sat up. As he uncurled, violet scent shook out from his body in clouds.

'Who is he?' Kit asked Juniper. 'He's not Dr Fell or Pig Woman. And does he look like a

Monster to you? Those labels must have been wrong.'

'I cry you mercy, master! But I *am* a Monster,' the boy said, his skinny chest swelling with pride. 'I am the Violet-Scented Boy. Come closer! My skin, my very sweat smells of violets. I am the most marvellous Monster at the fair!'

# Chapter Eight

That Violet-Scented Boy doesn't look very well, thought Kit.

He looked as frail and floppy as a newborn rabbit. His face was white and pinched, like a sick baby monkey's. And he was so weedy, he could hardly hold his head up. It seemed too big for his scrawny neck.

'You poorly?' Kit found himself asking. It must be a shock, being remade four hundred years in the future from your own smell molecules.

The Violet-Scented Boy didn't answer. His head drooped between his knees. Surely he couldn't be dozing again? But he'd jammed his toes in his ears. As well as being violet scented, he was extraordinarily bendy, like a rubber boy. He'd been an acrobat before he became a

Monster, twisting his body into all sorts of shapes.

It was a good job he could use his toes as earplugs. Or he'd never have got any sleep. Elizabethan fairs are very noisy places. Drums, pipes and trumpets compete with the cries of the stall owners, 'Buy my roast pig!' 'Buy my fine gingerbread!'

What a strange kid, thought Kit.

He was even worried about him, but what was the point of that? The E-Nose batteries would fail any second now. And, just like the Gladiator, the boy would become a shower of stars.

'Hey!' said Juniper suddenly. 'You can plug this machine in.'

'What?' said Kit, startled.

She'd found something underneath the E-Nose. 'It doesn't only work by batteries. There's a socket here.'

'Where're the wire and plug, though?'

'Don't know. Must still be in the box. Where are you going?'

Kit was already scooting up the cellar stairs. He didn't want the Violet-Scented Boy to break up in a sparkling blizzard of smell molecules. He wanted to know more about him.

What was it like, having sweat that smelled of violets? He'd sounded really proud of it: 'I am the most marvellous Monster at the fair!' At least he didn't stink like a skunk. But was it any better, ponging of violets? Just thinking about it made Kit's head spin.

He marvelled, 'That poor kid's got *serious* smell problems.' He felt strangely sympathetic. He wanted to talk to him some more.

He thought, If we plug in the E-Nose, we can keep him here.

Up in the kitchen, he rummaged in the box. 'Got it!' There was a plastic packet buried among the polystyrene beads. Inside it was a big coil of white wire with a plug on the end.

'Brilliant!' Kit stampeded downstairs into the cellar's gloom.

'The batteries are running low,' warned Juniper.

The Violet-Scented Boy was still asleep. But he was already surrounded by a haze of light. Those were his smell molecules, breaking loose.

Kit panted over to the E-Nose.

'We don't want *him* here!' said Juniper. 'I want Dr Fell. Then I want my dad!'

Wild ideas were whirling around in her brain. Now that they could plug in the E-Nose, there were possibilities she hadn't even dreamed of. Why couldn't Dad stay, not just for a few minutes, but for always?

Kit wasn't listening. He was frantically connecting up the E-Nose.

'Where can I plug it in?' he begged Juniper. It was almost too late.

'Up there,' said Juniper. 'Top of the steps, by the door.'

The Violet-Scented Boy was almost hidden in a cloud of stars. Had he already been disassembled? If he had, he was lost forever. There was no more Essence of Monster left.

Kit raced up the cellar steps. Would the wire stretch? Only just. He rammed the plug in the wall socket and flicked the switch to ON.

As the power from the mains surged through it, the E-Nose perked up. Its little green lights stopped fading. Now they glowed extra bright.

Kit came haring back down the steps. Had he been in time?

'Is he still here?'

The starry haze had gone. The Violet-Scented Boy slumbered on, not knowing he'd just been saved from being turned back into smell molecules.

Juniper came over to peer at him. He had a ragged brown tunic on, as rough and scratchy as a coal sack. And no shoes. His big toes were crammed in his ears. His spindly white arms hugged his skinny ribs. He looked pitiful. The powerful scent of violets rose from his whole body.

Kit said, 'Why did he call himself a Monster?'

Juniper answered vaguely. She was busy with other thoughts. 'Mum says they put people on display at Elizabethan fairs. You had to pay to see them. Sometimes it was a trick, like people who pretended to be mermaids or something. Sometimes they were poor people who couldn't help it. They'd been born like that. But they were still called Freaks or Monsters.'

'That's terrible!' said Kit. 'Well, I'm not going to call him a Monster. And Violet-Scented Boy sounds too sissy. I'm gonna call him the VSB,' he decided. 'That sounds better. So was he *born* smelling of violets?' he asked Juniper. 'Or was it a trick?'

'I don't know,' she said, hurrying back to the E-Nose. 'I just know you shouldn't be able to smell him.'

'What are you talking about? I don't get it.'

'That's cos you don't study smells, like I do. But try sniffing a violet. Its scent only lasts for about two seconds. Then it makes your nose numb. But he smells of violets *all the time*.'

'So?' said Kit. Trust a smell freak to think that was an interesting fact. As if the most important thing about him was his personal pong!

'I don't care what he *smells* like. I want to know about *him*!'

'Mum knows about him,' said Juniper, over her shoulder. 'She's got it on her computer. He had something to do with Dr Fell.'

Kit said, 'Can I ask your mum about him?' His dread of meeting Juniper's mum was still strong, but his curiosity about the VSB was stronger.

'No!' said Juniper impatiently. 'You're not even supposed to be here. But you can ask *Dr*

*Fell* if you like. After *I've* asked him about his  oil.'

'For heaven's sake! You're not still going to make him, are you?' asked Kit in alarm.

'Course,' said Juniper. 'I might have to have two tries though. I might make the Pig Woman first by mistake.'

'But now we've plugged in the E-Nose,' said Kit, 'that Dr Fell could be hanging around here forever!' What was wrong with her? Why couldn't she see it was dangerous?

'No, he won't,' Juniper insisted. 'When I find out what I want to know, I'll just switch off the machine. He'll get blasted back into smell molecules. Simple.'

'But you can't switch it off! The VSB will get blasted too!'

'What were you going to do with him anyway?' asked Juniper. 'Take him home? Adopt him or something?'

Kit had no idea. But he was saved from answering when a voice shouted from upstairs.

'Juniper!'

'It's your mum,' hissed Kit.

'Where've you got to?' the voice called again. 'Lunch is ready.'

'I'd better go,' said Juniper, 'before she comes looking.'

She whisked up the steps in a bright-green blur. Sequins and frills fell off her party frock. 'Don't touch anything. Promise!' she called back to Kit. 'I'll be back soon.'

Kit looked around the dungeon-like cellar. Strange floppings and scurryings came out of the darkness. He swallowed hard, twice. What have you got yourself into? he thought. He should head for home. Right now. But somehow he felt he had responsibilities.

It wasn't just Juniper. She could probably look after herself. Anyway, she could always ask her mum. But the VSB seemed so frail and helpless. Kit couldn't leave him. How could he cope in the twenty-first century?

'Poor little Monster,' he sighed, as he watched the VSB, trembling in his sleep like a puppy.

Then he had another thought, The computer!

Juniper's mum was having lunch in the kitchen.

I could nip up to her study now. I could find out more about him.

He thought of shaking the VSB awake and  taking him with him. But it would only slow him down. And the VSB looked like he needed his sleep.

Kit checked the E-Nose. What if it breaks down? he thought. What if someone switches it off? Or there's a power cut?

He might come back to find empty air where the VSB had been. But the E-Nose was still whirring away. How could a machine you could get on the Net have started such spooky events?

It wouldn't have been able to, thought Kit, without Dr Fell's special oil.

He shook himself. 'Better get moving. You haven't got much time.'

He galloped up the cellar steps again. As he passed, he checked that the plug was still pushed in. If that came out, the VSB was done for.

'He's a big worry, that VSB,' sighed Kit, closing the cellar door behind him. It was worse than trying to keep a baby bird alive. And he'd only been reassembled for about ten minutes!

There was a rusty bolt on the outside of the

cellar door. Kit hadn't noticed it before. He thought, Shall I lock him in? Then decided, No, he's not a prisoner.

He started tiptoeing up the back stairs to Juniper's mum's study.

Down in the cellar, there was silence for a moment. Except for the E-Nose, humming happily to itself.

Then a scrabbling came from a corner. It was the black rat, the one who'd almost been shipwrecked in his burger box, but had been saved by Kit's Gladiator can.

He was sick of stormy seas. He'd squeezed through a grille from the canal bank. It wasn't much drier in this cellar than out on the water, but at least the world wasn't heaving up and down.

He scuttled across the floor. He stopped to nibble the VSB's toe. Then he sneezed, '*Atisho!*' and leapt back. That violet scent was really disgusting. He liked his snacks to smell of sewers.

The VSB opened his bleary eyes. He raised his big, wobbly head.

'Pray you, stay, Master Rat,' he said. He needed some company. He was so lonely that even a rat was better than nothing.

But the rat couldn't stand his violet smell. It bounded off into the dark.

The VSB seemed to remember some other children being here. Strange, foreign-looking children. But he had been half asleep. 'I pray they may come again,' he whispered. Perhaps they could be friends.

Suddenly his face twisted with pain. 'My guts are wringing!' said the Violet-Scented Boy, hugging his aching belly.

He didn't know why he'd been so sick lately. So sleepy all the time.

He felt his eyelids drooping. He peered woozily into the dark. He didn't know he was in the cellar of 19 Canal Street, in the twenty-first century. As far as he was concerned, he was still in Elizabethan times, in the dark, damp kitchen of Dr Fell's house, where he'd been held prisoner for two days and nights.

Before he fell asleep again, he mumbled something. It was a plea to the Pig Woman, who sold greasy roast pork at the fair.

'Are you *sure* Dr Fell is a fine gentleman? He makes me turn a spit. He shouts, "*Sweat, noddle, sweat!*" I am sore afraid. Oh, when shall you come and rescue me, Mother?'

# Chapter Nine

As he climbed, Kit caught a whiff of burnt breadcrumbs. And was that bacon, crisping under the grill? Toasted bacon sarnies! The thought made his empty belly gurgle.

'Shut up,' he told it, as he opened the door to Juniper's mum's study.

He pushed his way past the titan arum. It was so lush and jungly, it looked ready to take over the whole study. But he hardly glanced at its huge, swollen flower bud. He had other things on his mind.

There was some writing on the computer:

'Kids!' it said. 'Ever heard of Love Apples? In Elizabethan times, a young girl in love would tuck a peeled apple into her armpit. She'd leave it there for a few hours, then give it to her boyfriend as a present, so he could smell her  even when they were apart. Isn't that romantic? Why don't boyfriends and girlfriends do that these days? Don't you think it's time to bring back this charming old custom?'

'*Euch!*' shuddered Kit, quickly clicking on *Exit*. 'Is this woman totally round the bend?'

He searched through some other file names. Most of them made no sense. There was nothing about the Violet-Scented Boy. Then he came across one that said 'Dr Fell'.

'Found you, Old No-Nose,' breathed Kit.

He clicked the mouse and brought the file on the screen.

Frantically, he started reading. Juniper's mum might come back at any moment.

'*Aarrrgh!*' He jumped a mile. But it was only the titan arum, flopping one of its leaves over his shoulder. Kit brushed it off.

'*Concentrate, concentrate,*' he told himself, through gritted teeth. But most of this was scientific stuff, that only smell experts could understand.

At last! Here was a bit about the VSB. Kit read it greedily. Then sighed in exasperation. It was just about violet scent.

'Violets numb the nose after a few seconds of smelling . . .' Juniper's mum had written.

I already know that, thought Kit, amazed that he knew something.

'. . . so it's very hard to make a violet scent that lasts,' he read on. 'Queen Elizabeth even offered a prize to all her scent makers. "Whoever makes Essence of Violets shall please me mightily," the Queen said.'

'Wait a minute!' Connections were being made in Kit's brain. Then there it was, staring at him from the screen.

'After his false-nose fiasco, Dr Fell was desperate to get back in Queen Elizabeth's good books,' Juniper's mum had written. 'He decided that making her a violet perfume was the perfect way to do it. He'd heard of a Monster at a travelling fair whose skin and sweat smelled of violets. It's said that Dr Fell kidnapped the boy so he could use his smell.'

Kit read it again. The words on the screen seemed to scorch into his brain. 'Dr Fell kidnapped the VSB. To steal his smell. That's criminal,' he whispered.

But Kit shouldn't have been surprised. It was typical of Dr Fell. He was a ruthless

person. If he wanted anything, he took it.
Jockstraps from gladiator's graves. Noses from
dead people. Smells from children. He just
didn't care.

Kit heard voices far below him. Time to go.

Juniper's mum mustn't know that someone
had been sneaking a look at her notes. Kit
tried to find the file that had been on the
screen, but he clicked on the wrong one. His
hands were shaking so much because of the
shocking things he'd just learned.

Something else came up on the screen. It
was about Juniper.

'Get out of here! NOW!' his brain was
screaming at him. But he couldn't help
snatching a quick look.

'My experiment in bringing up my
daughter, Juniper, has been one hundred per
cent successful. I have proved it can be done!
In the interests of smell research, I have raised
a child *entirely without smell prejudice*.'

Juniper an *experiment*? But Kit didn't have
time to think about that. He hit a few more
keys. At last, the stuff about Love Apples came
up again on the screen.

*Phew!* thought Kit, wiping his face.

He went tearing down the back way to the cellar. Just in time. He heard Juniper's mum say, 'Back to the grindstone!' Caught a flash of her purple boots as she clanged up the iron staircase to her study.

Surely she'd noticed that violet smell? It seemed to be spreading through the whole factory. It had even driven out the smell of cat food.

'See you later, Mum,' said Juniper's voice.

'MUM!' thought Kit, skidding to a stop. His own mum would be wondering where he'd got to. Time to check in. He took out his mobile and gave her a call.

'Mum, it's me. Yes, I'm OK. I'm round a mate's house. Yes, yes, yes, yes, yes, yes.'

He was just about to cut her off before she asked any more awkward questions, then something to ask *her* suddenly popped into his head.

'Mum,' he said, 'could you recognize me just by sniffing my sweaty T-shirt? Pardon? What do you mean, "*Do I have to*"?'

He put his phone away. For a second, all his old smell insecurities came flooding back. But he couldn't worry about them now. He had to get down to the cellar to see if the VSB was all  right. Plus, he was bursting with news to tell Juniper.

She was waiting in the gloom. How long had she been here?

'I've got loads to tell you,' said Kit. 'Stuff I found out about the VSB.'

He'd already decided not to mention what he'd read on the computer screen about her. I wouldn't like it, he thought, being brought up as an *experiment*.

But first he dashed over to the E-Nose. Its green lights were still glowing. 'Thank goodness,' breathed Kit.

That meant the VSB was still here. He'd been scared to look before. He hurried over to see him.

The VSB was shivering himself awake. He raised his tatty head, took his big toes out of his ears and stretched like a hamster waking up. He stared up at Kit with big, bewildered eyes.

'Are you Dr Fell's servant?'

'No way!' said Kit, indignantly. 'I hate that slimeball, that Smell Stealer!'

The VSB looked shocked.

'But Mother says Dr Fell is a fine gentleman.'

'Mother?' said Kit. It had somehow never occurred to him that the poor little Monster had a mother.

'Mother keeps pigs. She roasts them at the fair.'

'The Pig Woman!' said Juniper, who had been strangely silent up to now.

'But I beg you, gentle sir, tell her where I am,' said the VSB. 'I was stolen away.'

'I know,' said Kit grimly.

The VSB was getting over his fear. He was even becoming chatty. He was quite used to strangers. Every day, he sat in a booth while crowds of people paid to sniff him. 'Draw near, my masters!' the Pig Woman would cry. 'Smell my Violet-Scented Boy. The Queen herself would give a gold-filled purse to sniff such a perfume!'

'I turned the spit in Dr Fell's kitchen,' the VSB told Kit. 'The fire was roaring! He cries to me, "*Sweat, noddle, sweat!*"'

Kit threw a meaningful look at Juniper. 'Dr Fell was collecting his sweat,' he hissed out the corner of his mouth, 'for Queen Elizabeth.'

'He called me *noddle* and *blockhead*!'  complained the VSB. His wrinkly little old man's face was screwed up in outrage. 'But I am a famous Monster! At your service, master and mistress.'

The VSB scrambled to his feet and made a low, sweeping bow. Then went floppy and fell forward on to his nose.

'I have a weakness in my legs,' he moaned.

In the darkness, Juniper coughed quietly, as if she wanted to tell Kit something.

But Kit was too busy saying to the VSB, 'Don't worry, you're safe. You've got friends now. That Dr Fell scumbag can't get you here.'

He was considering telling the VSB the whole story. How he'd been reassembled from his smell molecules. Only he wasn't sure where to start. And wouldn't the shock be too much for such a frail child?

Then Juniper coughed again. '*A-hem!*'

'What's up?' said Kit at last, turning his head.

A sudden sound came out of the darkness. *Clink!*

There was a muffled curse. Something gleaming came hopping over the flagstones and stopped at Kit's feet. It was a false nose.

'It's him!' cried the VSB, sounding panic-stricken.

He screwed his rubbery body into a ball again and plugged his big toes in his ears.

# Chapter Ten

Kit's whole body was suddenly freezing, as if he'd been plunged in an icy pool.

'Tell me you didn't!' he gasped at Juniper. 'You didn't make *Dr Fell*?'

Nobody spoke in the cellar. All you could hear was the soft humming of the E-Nose. And the *slap, slap, slap* of canal water against the cellar walls.

In his own little curled-up world, the VSB didn't hear Kit's question. He was thinking about the first time he and his mum, the Pig Woman, had met Dr Fell.

Dr Fell had turned up long after the fair had closed. He'd suddenly swooped out of the darkness.

His mum was sitting among her pigs, smoking her clay pipe. He'd been poorly as usual. He was eating the wild lettuce soup that Mum cooked him every day. 'It will make you into a fine, strong lad,' she'd promised.

Dr Fell had said, 'Sweet Mistress Pig Woman, I have heard talk of your famous Monster. How he smells most strongly of violets.'

'He does indeed, sir,' said the Pig Woman, dropping a curtsey.

Dr Fell had put his gold false nose on, just to impress her. He was wearing a black velvet hat and cloak. The cloak was wrapped round him, so he looked like a giant bat.

He'd asked for a special smelling.

The Pig Woman had almost said, 'Smell him? But you've got no nose!'

But she'd kept quiet because he'd paid a whole sixpence.

He'd said, 'Your Monster is indeed a marvel. I shall come again to smell him.'

The Pig Woman was thrilled. 'What a generous gentleman!' she'd giggled, after he'd gone. 'Methinks he's taken quite a fancy to me!'

Next time he came, she'd decided, she would make a big effort. She would scrape the pork grease off her face. And wear an apron that wasn't all crusty with pig poo. And put the  price up to a shilling.

The VSB whimpered. He closed his eyes tighter and tried to pretend he was safe at home, scoffing a bowl of his mum's wild lettuce soup. He hadn't liked it much before, but now he wanted it more than anything.

'You made him, didn't you?' Kit hissed again to Juniper.

Juniper had heard his question the first time. But she still didn't answer it. She was too busy working out how to handle Dr Fell.

'Just ask him about his special oil. Then switch off the E-Nose and blast him back into smell molecules. It's easy,' she told herself.

But her mouth felt bone dry. She swallowed hard, twice. This wasn't like reassembling the Gladiator – he had about two brain cells. Dr Fell was much riskier. He was a Master Swordsman *and* a Master of Smells. And, oh yes, she'd almost forgotten. He was also a kidnapper, a grave robber and a big fan of gruesome nose-grafting experiments.

But what else could she do? If there was the tiniest chance of getting her dad back, she had to take it.

Kit didn't need to ask his question a third time. He could see the answer for himself. There was an empty vial by the E-Nose.

'Where is he?' whispered Kit.

There was only a dim pool of light. Most of the cellar was swallowed up in darkness. It had dozens of drippy, frog-filled nooks and crannies. You could hide out here for days.

Kit couldn't see him, but Dr Fell was very close. He was crouched in the gloom, gluing on a spare nose. He always carried some in a pouch hanging from his belt. He put his glue pot away. Then pulled out his rapier.

The Master Swordsman had got a bit rusty since his duelling days, but he was still as light on his feet as a cat.

'What mischief is this?' said a gravelly voice, right into Kit's ear.

Kit whirled round. '*AAAARGH!*'

At first, all he could see were two twin points of light. They were the tips of Dr Fell's silver nose and his sword. Then Old No-Nose himself stepped out of the shadows.

Juniper gasped. Her hand flew to her mouth. What had she done?

He looked grotesque. Only a Pig Woman

could find him attractive. At Court, he'd been Queen Elizabeth's favourite. But since then he'd let himself go – a lot.

For a start, his nose was on askew. It was hard to fix it straight without a mirror. Once he'd been fashionable, dressed in the finest clothes. He'd had the most starched ruff in town, but now it was all droopy. His gold lacy cuffs were decayed. And was that grave mould on his cloak?

'You are thieves!' he cried, in a voice as raspy as a cheese grater.

Under his black velvet hat, his eyes glittered with menace. He didn't seem to mind where he was. Only two things mattered to him.

1. Finding himself the perfect new nose
2. Getting back into Queen Elizabeth's good books

'You are Foreigners,' said Dr Fell, staring at their strange clothes, 'come to steal my Monster. His violet scent is *mine*! When she smells it, Queen Elizabeth shall make me a lord!'

He flung back his head and laughed, '*Ha,*

*ha, ha!*' His metal nose flew off and clinked into a corner.

'Curses!'

Dr Fell dived back into the shadows to glue on a new one.

Kit had heard that kind of laugh before. It was the mad, cackling laugh you hear in horror films. The laugh of someone who's gone right off his rocker.

'You just said he went a bit funny,' Kit hissed to Juniper. 'You didn't say he was completely insane!'

Dr Fell sprang out of the darkness, rapier at the ready. This time he'd stuck on a gold, party-going nose. He wouldn't usually wear it to kill rogues like these. A wooden nose was all they were worth, but he didn't have one handy.

Trembling, Juniper stepped forward.

'Dr Fell,' she said, in a shaky voice. 'Please can you tell me what's in your special oil? The one you preserve smells in?'

Dr Fell turned his burning gaze upon her. She felt it might shrivel her up.

'Lizards' gizzards,' said Dr Fell, 'and unicorn horn and powdered mermaid's hair.'

I couldn't make that, thought Juniper. She

felt those precious bubbles of hope going pop, one by one.

'And many other secret ingredients,' said Dr Fell, cunningly, 'but without the right spells the oil will not work.'

Spells? thought Juniper, totally bewildered. Was he telling the truth? Was he lying through his teeth? Or was he just as crazy as a coot?

'You mean you use *magic*?' asked Juniper. 'As well as science?'

Her plan of remaking her dad was crumbling to ashes.

Dr Fell didn't seem to understand the question. To him, magic and science weren't separate.

'What spells?' Juniper found herself asking.

There was a long, warning hiss from Kit. That hiss said, 'For heaven's sake! Haven't you gone far enough?'

Dr Fell thought so too. 'You scurvy knaves! You come to steal my Monster, then seek to know my secret spells. Torture would not make me tell you!'

His rapier whizzed and slashed. He was just getting warmed up. It left whirls of light in the dark, like a sparkler.

He sprang forward. The sword swished past Kit's ear. He could feel the rush of wind.

'Now I shall chop you into gobbets,' said Dr Fell. He sounded as if he was going to enjoy it.

*Clink*

'A plague on these noses!' cried Dr Fell.

But this time he didn't retreat into the shadows. He didn't even sheath his sword.

'Do not stir!' Dr Fell warned them.

He pulled his cloak over his face and fumbled about. He was very nifty at one-handed nose replacement.

Kit's brain told him, 'Run!'

But there was no point trying to escape – Dr Fell would run you through before you reached the cellar steps.

No one noticed but the VSB was uncurling from his egg shape. He peeped though his long, bony fingers.

'I'm switching off the E-Nose,' said Juniper suddenly.

At last she'd admitted it to herself. Meeting her dad again wasn't going to happen. She'd been stupid to have those hopes. And Dr Fell was far too dangerous to have around.

'No, wait,' whispered Kit.

What's happening? thought Juniper. She'd finally come to her senses, but Kit seemed to be the crazy one now!

'He's going to kill us,' hissed Juniper, reaching out for the OFF switch.

'What about the VSB? You'll blast him too!'

Too bad! thought Juniper grimly, as Dr Fell swirled aside his cloak and crouched in a swordsman's stance. In those tight black stockings, his legs looked as springy as a cricket's.

What nose had he glued on now? It wasn't silver or gold. It was black and withered, like the noses that poke through mummies' bandages.

It can't be! thought Kit, horrified. But he had no time to be disgusted.

'Prepare to die!' Dr Fell told them.

Through his fingers, the VSB saw what was happening. He thought, I must save my friends from this murderer!

Then he spoke. Everyone's eyes turned towards him. He was so scared of Dr Fell that his tiny frame shook like a flag flapping in the wind.

'Good Dr Fell,' his voice trembled, 'do not

forget. You have important business in the graveyard.'

'You are right, noddle!' cried Dr Fell. He lowered his sword. 'I need some more noses!' He hadn't had much luck so far, but he was still keen on nose grafting. If it worked, it would be the perfect solution to his problems. Maybe his stolen noses just hadn't been fresh enough . . .

'I wonder if there's a funeral today!' he said excitedly. 'These foreign thieves must await my pleasure. But you, Monster, shall come with me.'

'Pray you, Dr Fell!' shuddered the VSB. 'Let me stay here! Graveyards do not agree with me.'

'Are you sick again?' said Dr Fell, poking his shrivelled conk close to the boy.

Dr Fell didn't want the VSB dying on him. He needed him to stay alive so he could collect his violet essence.

'No, sir, no,' the VSB assured him.

In fact, apart from his fear, he felt a lot stronger. Better than he'd felt since last spring, when he'd started to smell of violets.

But, as his strength returned, his violet smell

seemed to be fading. He sniffed his armpit, secretly. Why had no one noticed except himself?

'This poxy nose,' said Dr Fell. 'I could not smell a sewer with it.'

Suddenly, as if he could read the VSB's mind, Dr Fell said suspiciously, 'Tell me, noddle, is your violet scent as strong?'

'Yes, sir, yes,' lied the VSB, scrambling up on his pipe-cleaner legs and throwing out his weedy arms. 'See me, sir! I am the famous Violet-Scented Boy. The Whole World flocks to see me! My smell will never fade!'

'*Hmmmm,*' said Dr Fell, but for the moment he seemed to believe him.

The VSB was a sick boy. But he wasn't stupid. He knew that without his violet smell he was useless to Dr Fell. And he knew too that Dr Fell wouldn't just give a cheery wave and cry, 'Farewell! You're free to go back to the fair!'

But Dr Fell had already snatched him up. He went bounding up the cellar steps with the VSB tucked under his arm like a French loaf. The cellar door slammed shut.

Kit and Juniper heard the rusty iron bolt slide across.

They stared at each other.

'He's locked us in,' said Kit. 'So what are we going to do now?'

# Chapter Eleven

'Aren't you going to say, "Let's switch off the E-Nose"?' Kit asked Juniper.

The E-Nose was still humming away to itself. It looked like a toaster lit up with fairy lights.

How could that little machine have caused all this trouble? thought Kit.

But Juniper had changed her mind about cutting the power. If she blasted Dr Fell into his smell molecules, then the VSB would go too. They owed him more than that.

'That VSB just saved our lives,' she said.

'It was a brave thing he did,' agreed Kit. 'Butting in like that. Dr Fell was going to turn us into dog meat.'

'We've *got* to get the VSB away from him,' said Juniper.

'Oh yeah? How?'

'*Some*how,' insisted Juniper.

She looked as stubborn about it as she'd been about bringing back her dad. But Kit wasn't going to argue. He'd felt a strange bond with the VSB ever since he learned about his smell problems.

'We'd better get out of this cellar for a start,' said Kit, 'before Dr Fell comes back.'

Then he had an idea. 'We could call your mum on my mobile. Say, "Help! Come and let us out."'

'No!' said Juniper. 'I don't want her to know what I've been doing.'

'You've got to tell her *sometime*,' said Kit. 'What happens when she needs those smells for her scratch-and-sniff book? And there's only Essence of Pig Woman left?'

Juniper felt in her pocket. The Pig Woman's vial was still there. Along with the fragment of her dad's furry mitten and the tape of his smell profile. But they didn't make up for not meeting her dad in person. Not when she'd longed for it so desperately.

'Stop thinking about it!' her brain ordered her. 'IT'S NOT GOING TO HAPPEN.'

'Come on,' she said to Kit. 'I know a way  out.' She plunged into the blackness.

The rat scuttled past her. He'd recovered now from almost being shipwrecked. He looked frisky and alert. The only trouble was, he was feeling peckish. He sniffed at the white wire dangling from underneath the E-Nose. He clicked his needle-sharp teeth. Was he going to have a nibble? No. He liked his food to smell stinkier. He might come back to it later.

'How can you see where you're going?' said Kit, trying to keep up with Juniper. She was just a green blur in the gloom. 'It's like midnight down here! *Ow!*' He'd just skinned his ankle on something sharp. He couldn't even see what it was. He reached down to rub his leg.

'*Ugh,*' He'd touched something cold and slimy. *Kerroak!* It hopped off into the dark.

'I don't have to see,' said Juniper. 'I can smell. Just stay close to me.'

She flung herself on to the stone floor and sniffed. 'I'm looking for the rat path,' she said. 'They come in here from outside.' She sniffed some more. 'Got it! Come on.'

She wriggled away, with Kit shuffling behind, hanging on to one of her trailing frills. He didn't want to get lost. It was like a maze down here.

Juniper sniffed again. 'Here's the toad corner,' she said. 'We're going the right way.'

*Plop.* Something landed on Kit's shoe. He shook it off. Rat, toad, or frog, he had no idea. Juniper would have been able to tell him. But she was sniffing somewhere else. And he'd let go of the frill. He spun round helplessly in the dark.

'Careful!'

He'd almost tripped over her.

*Phew!* thought Kit, relieved. You nearly lost her that time.

They went slowly through the cellar, with Juniper finding her way by smell. She sniffed rusty pipes and old tar barrels. She stopped again.

'What are you smelling now?' asked Kit.

'Ferns growing out of the wall.'

Kit couldn't even see them. But when he put his hand out, a frondy leaf tickled it.

'What do ferns smell like?'

'Oh,' said Juniper vaguely, 'they smell of

forests. They smell ... sort of green and woody.' She sniffed again, concentrating. 'We're nearly there! I can smell the canal!'

Even Kit could smell it now. That mixture of fishy mud, oily water and rotting rubbish.

'Wait a minute,' said Kit. 'You've been this way before, haven't you?'

'Course I have,' came a voice out of the dark. 'How else do you think I got this smell map in my head?'

She didn't give any more details. But lately, when 19 Canal Street got too claustrophobic, when she needed to escape from her mum for a while, she'd sneak out this way without her knowing. She liked to do it at night. Best of all were the clear nights when the moon was full. Then the canal and all the ruins round it seemed like a white wilderness. Everything was frozen in silver stillness.

I'm in the Arctic, she would imagine, looking around, smiling. The smell-less Arctic. Where no one would think she was weird.

'There's light up there!' said Kit. At last he could see where he was going. 'There are some stairs. Is this the way out?'

But Juniper was already crawling up the

stone steps and unbolting the big metal grille at the top.

Kit scrambled out on to the canal bank. He blinked in the dazzling sunshine. 'Where now?' he said, looking around.

There was no sign of Dr Fell or the VSB.

'Think they're still in the house?' asked Kit. But the front door of 19 Canal Street stood wide open.

'No, I think he's gone to find a graveyard,' said Juniper.

Up in her study, Juniper's mum was tapping away at *The Wonderful World of Smells*. She'd nearly finished it. Then she'd be starting her scratch-and-sniff book, *Find Out What People From the Past* Really *Smelled Like*.

Thinking about it made her reach out and pat Dr Fell's Cabinet of Human Smells. She almost opened it, just so she could gaze at the four vials she was going to use: the Essences of Monster, Pig Woman, Gladiator and the great Dr Thomas Fell himself. Pity she didn't know the names of the first three. She'd probably never find out who they were.

When is that E-Nose going to turn up? she

wondered. Then she could get the recipes for these ancient smells. Have them made up again, in bucket loads, just as smelly as when they were brand new.

She started pulling out the top tray. Then she slapped her hand away.

'No,' she scolded herself, 'finish this book first!'

She turned back to the screen.

She was writing a chapter called The World's Smelliest Plants. She'd already done the titan arum, of course. And the voodoo lily, that smelled like rotting meat. Now she was surfing the Net, looking for some more examples.

Suddenly she leaned forward in her chair and peered closely at the screen.

'WILD LETTUCE,' it said, '(*Lactuca virosa*), commonly grows in woodland. This type of lettuce, unlike garden lettuce, is POISONOUS. Two of the symptoms are weakness and sleepiness. It also, because of chemicals it contains, makes the victim smell of violets. If eaten regularly, extreme sickness will result and eventually DEATH.'

Juniper's mum read it again. Then she

leaned back. 'Hummm,' she murmured. 'Wild lettuce? Makes you smell of violets? At the same time as it's poisoning you? That's weird.'

But it wasn't what she was looking for. So she surfed right past it.

# Chapter Twelve

I f Dr Fell was looking for graveyards around here, he wasn't going to have much luck.

'I can't see any cemeteries,' said Kit. There were only wrecked buildings and barbed wire. It looked like an old bomb site, taken over by weeds, with a scummy canal flowing through it.

Juniper crouched down on the towpath. She sniffed around, like a bloodhound, searching for a scent.

Kit didn't have to ask. He knew she was trying to track the VSB.

'That's strange,' she said, shaking her head. 'His violet smell isn't as strong as it was before.'

'Hold the Pig Woman's vial,' she told Kit. 'So it doesn't get broken.' Kit stashed it away carefully in his pocket.

Juniper threw herself full length on the path. She put her nose close to the soil and snuffled up the smells. She wriggled along a bit, like a bright-green snake. She sniffed some more.

This time Kit wasn't even slightly shocked by her behaviour.

So what's wrong with being a smell freak? he found himself thinking. After all, Freddie's a *taste* freak.

Freddie, his baby brother, tasted everything. He licked worms, he sucked the dog's blanket, he ate dirt out of cracks in the pavement. Being a smell freak wasn't half so disgusting, Kit decided. In fact, it seemed perfectly normal. Especially when it was helping you find a missing person.

Every time Kit thought of the poor VSB in the clutches of Dr Fell, he shuddered. The guy was a ghoul!

'Old No-Nose, Old Smell Stealer! We're coming to get you!'

Kit spat out the words. But it didn't make him feel much better. Even just *thinking* about Dr Fell scared him. What was it like for the VSB, staring straight into that madman's eyes above his shrivelled Egyptian-mummy nose?

'Have you picked up the trail yet?' he asked Juniper anxiously. 'He's getting away.'

Juniper sprang to her feet. Showers of sequins pinged off her princess frock. She'd suddenly remembered something. Why was she gazing into the distance?

'We don't need a smell trail,' she said. 'Look!'

Kit followed her pointing finger. Above the crumbling factories he saw a wonky spire with the top missing.

'It's a church!' said Kit.

'I forgot about it,' said Juniper. 'It's practically fallen down.'

'Did it have a graveyard?'

'Don't know,' said Juniper. 'But if *we* can see the spire from here, so could Dr Fell. I bet that's where he's heading.'

'Come on then,' said Kit, breaking into a run. They were a long way behind. He just hoped that Dr Fell had stopped somewhere to glue on another false nose.

Dr Fell slashed his way through some tall purple weeds. *Sssss!* His sword hissed through the air. The heads of some big white daisies went flying.

*What great catastrophe has happened here?* he thought.

The town was in ruins. All the townsfolk had fled.

Was it war, plague, or fire? Whatever it was, the graveyard would be stuffed with bodies.

*Perfect for my purposes,* thought Dr Fell gleefully.

But how had he been transported here? He suspected sorcery. None of that mattered though. To his mad brain they were mere details. His nose quest was much more important.

'Make haste!' he said to the VSB, who was plodding behind him. He looked up at the church spire to get his bearings. 'This way!'

Robbing graves in an empty town was child's play. You didn't have to sneak about with a spade in the dark. You could do it in broad daylight. Things were looking up.

*Plop.* 'Curses,' fumed Dr Fell. His last spare nose had dropped off.

For a few seconds, a shocked VSB saw a skull-like face with a hole in the centre. Then Dr Fell tied a black silky hanky over it so he looked like a highwayman. But he still wasn't downhearted.

'I have great hopes,' he raved to the VSB, 'that we shall soon be back in London! Her Majesty shall make me Lord High Scent Maker. And all those who mocked me will be quaking in their boots!'

The VSB stumbled along behind him. His belly felt better, but he was still in despair. He had no idea that Kit and Juniper were hot on their trail. He believed he'd been abandoned. His mother, the Pig Woman, didn't even know where he was.

In London, he thought, I shall be a prisoner! I shall have to turn a spit before a roaring fire until my sweat runs down in rivers!

What kind of life was that for a famous Monster?

He thought about running away. Bit by bit, he was feeling better. But he wasn't strong enough yet, and he knew he wouldn't get very far before Dr Fell caught him. Besides, he had no idea where he was. He looked around, with big, scared eyes.

'What strange, bewitched place is this?' he whispered to himself. It seemed like the end of the world. How could Mother find him here?

He thought about how Dr Fell had tricked them.

It was very hard to trick the Pig Woman. She was a wise and cunning person. But when she was in love, her brains went right out the window.

'He has begged me for a Love Apple!' she had said to the VSB, tucking a peeled apple into her hairy armpit. 'I told you he fancied me!'

Dr Fell had also asked the VSB for a piece of his tunic. 'I shall preserve *both* your smells,' he'd told them, 'in my special oil.' He'd made them feel really important.

Then one night he'd struck, swift as a snake. The Pig Woman trusted him. She'd gone off to collect wild lettuce in the woods, peacefully smoking her clay pipe and had left him alone to look after the VSB.

'You are mine now, you scurvy little Monster,' Dr Fell had cried, as soon as the Pig Woman's back was turned. Then he'd bundled the VSB up in his black cloak and whisked him away.

The last thing the VSB had heard was his mother, wailing aloud in her grief, 'Oh, where are you, my Violet-Scented Boy?'

While Juniper, Kit, Dr Fell and the VSB all headed for the church spire, Juniper's mum, up in her study, had a big stretch.

'Hurray!' she cried out loud. 'Finished!' She had just typed the very last sentence of *The Wonderful World of Smells*.

She relaxed for a bit. She took a swig of coffee, then turned round to admire the titan arum. When that bud burst, it would be a big event. The whole house would be full of its odour. Some people would need gas masks just to step inside!

Wimps, thought Juniper's mum. She was a smell warrior. The worse other people found a smell, the more she liked it.

Juniper's mum was a fidgety person, full of energy. 'That's enough time off,' she told herself.

She pulled Dr Fell's Cabinet of Human Smells towards her.

'These four vials are absolutely priceless,' she murmured to herself as she slid out the top tray.

# Chapter Thirteen

Juniper stopped and sniffed the wind. They were very close to the church now.

'I smell buried bodies,' said Juniper.

'What?' said Kit, shocked.

'It's just a whiff of mouldy old bones,' Juniper explained. 'Skeletons, I should think. I'd be surprised if they had any noses left.'

Kit's stomach gave a tiny, sick flip. Once again, he was amazed by how unsqueamish Juniper was. Dead, decaying things, rottenness, stinks of all sorts – she took them all in her stride.

It was very comforting to someone who was insecure about his smell. Not that Kit had thought about that much lately.

He sniffed his armpit secretly. It was hours since that last squirt of Gladiator.

Hey! he thought, pleased. I don't smell too bad!

'Too bad compared to what?' said that sarcastic voice inside his head. 'A putrefying whale washed up on a beach? An egg sandwich that's been left in your lunch box, inside your school backpack, since the last day of term?'

*Whoops*, thought Kit, suddenly reminded. I must take that out when I get home.

But this was no time to worry about trivial stuff.

He had other, more urgent, things on his mind. Matters of life and death. Like a sick boy, kidnapped by a crazy Elizabethan smell freak and Master Swordsman.

He'd better not hurt the VSB, thought Kit.

The VSB seemed so fragile, as if a puff of wind could blow him over. You couldn't help wanting to protect him.

'There's the church,' said Juniper as they squeezed through some iron railings.

The church was a wreck. Its stained-glass windows were shattered. Pigeons fluttered in and out through holes in the wall. Someone had sprayed graffiti all over the doors.

'Do you think they're in there?' Kit asked Juniper.

She sniffed. Then frowned and nodded. 'I can smell violets,' she said.

'So what do we do now?' asked Kit.

Dr Fell was mad. But he was also deadly. Anyone who tried to steal his Monster would end up leakier than a sieve.

Even Juniper shivered. The thought of that black, swirling cloak, that detachable conk, made her cold with dread.

'We can't leave the VSB with him,' she whispered. 'Dr Fell's the *real* monster.'

'I'm going inside,' said Kit suddenly. 'You stay here. Keep watch. In case they come out another way.'

Then he did a really startling thing. He even surprised himself. He screwed his fist around in his armpit, then clasped her wrist. 'Essence of Me,' he said. 'Catch you later.'

He disappeared through the church doors.

Kit stared up, his mouth hanging open. There was no roof! Like a Roman arena, the old church was open to the sky. He could see blue sky up there, birds swooping by.

His eyes darted around, checking for Dr Fell

and the VSB. The inside of the church was stripped bare. Only the walls were left, with a sort of wooden balcony clinging to them. But Dr Fell wasn't up there. Where was the old Smell Snatcher?

Kit started to search. He kept close to the walls.

At some time, the church had been used to store builder's materials. There were torn sacks in corners, sand all over the floor.

'*Ow!*'

Kit swore softly. He'd just stabbed his hand on a splintered plank. He licked at a bright-red bead of blood.

Maybe they're not here at all, he thought.

He stopped hugging the walls and moved cautiously out into the big, airy space.

He felt like a sitting duck. He could hear his own heartbeat. *Boom, boom, boom.* It seemed to echo around the church.

Kit stepped past the drum of an old cement mixer sitting on the floor.

I can smell violets, he thought suddenly.

He crouched down. And there was the VSB, curled up inside the drum, like a dormouse in its nest. He had his toes jammed in his ears. He was pretending he was back with his mum. Eating a hot, steamy bowlful of her wild lettuce soup. He just knew that would make him feel better.

Kit put his head inside the drum and unplugged one grubby toe.

'Where's that crazy guy gone?' he whispered, right into the VSB's ear.

The VSB's shaggy head jerked up. His wide, scared eyes scanned Kit's face.

'Master, I beg you. Do not stay here!'

'I'm not your master,' hissed Kit. 'I'm just another kid, like you. And I'm going to get you out of here! Come on!'

The VSB spilled out on to the sandy floor, like a slippery white lizard.

'I dare not! I dare not! He told me, "DO NOT STIR!"'

'So where is he?' asked Kit again, his heart *booming* even louder than before.

The VSB gave a low moan. 'He said, "I am off to seek noses."'

He pointed a shaky finger. Kit saw a great hole in the church floor, with stone steps leading down. 'He has gone down there.'

The VSB gazed fearfully at the gaping hole.

To him it seemed like the gateway to hell. For all he knew, Dr Fell could be a demon. He could be the Devil himself.

Kit knew better. He knew about crypts under churches from old horror films.

'I bet there're coffins down there, and tombs and stuff,' he told the VSB. That would keep the old grave robber busy.

Down in the dark crypt, Dr Fell was cursing. 'I have not found me one poxy nose!'

He was looking for fresh bodies – well, fairly fresh ones anyway. But there weren't even skeletons here. Any bones and stone coffins had been cleared out years ago. What Juniper had sniffed on the wind was Dr Fell's personal smell profile. All that decaying finery and graveyard mould meant he stunk of death all the time.

'Come on!' said Kit, grabbing the VSB's scraggy arm. 'We've got to make a run for it. While we've got the chance.'

They were too slow. As the VSB wobbled to his feet, a head seemed to rise from the floor. It hardly seemed human. Between the black velvet hat and black mask, all you could see were two eyes, burning with hatred. It was the old grave robber himself.

'I spy – a thief!' rasped the head. 'How did you escape?'

Dr Fell sprang out of the crypt, rapier at the ready.

He turned his scorching gaze on the VSB. 'Or do I smell *conspiracy* here? Is this some rogue from the fair come to free you?'

'Have mercy on us!' cried the VSB.

Kit frantically tried to think. Words came bursting out of his mouth. 'He's no use to you anyway!'

The VSB wanted to warn him, 'Don't say that!' He tried to tug at Kit's arm. But he was so weedy it was like being brushed by a humming bird.

Kit carried on. 'You only want to steal his smell, but he hardly smells of violets now. So you might as well set him free.'

Above his mask, Dr Fell's mad eyes narrowed to gleaming slits.

'Does he speak the truth?' he asked the VSB in his throaty voice. 'Because if he does, alas, I shall have to run you both through.'

He whipped his sword round his head in a

glittering circle. The VSB screwed himself up,  snail-tight.

'No!' cried Kit as the sword came slashing down. But it only sliced off a tuft of the VSB's hair.

'I was lying!' babbled Kit. 'I just wanted you to let him go.'

'You were trying to cheat me!' hissed Dr Fell in a rage. 'A poor unfortunate who has no nose and cannot smell for himself. You shall pay for that!'

He threw back his head and gave his lunatic laugh. It scared the pigeons roosting on top of the walls. They swirled like a white blizzard into the sky.

It also alerted Juniper. She'd been on her way in anyway. She couldn't stand it a moment longer, waiting outside, trying to smell what was going on.

She peeped round the door. She summed up the situation in two seconds flat.

He's got them trapped! she thought.

She couldn't think clearly. Her head felt like a cave full of flapping bats.

I've got to switch off the E-Nose, she decided. Blast Dr Fell into smell molecules.

She didn't want to do it. It meant sacrificing the VSB. But at least Kit would be safe and, besides, she couldn't think of any other solution.

She started running, stumbling over rubble, tearing her princess frock. She left a trail of sequins like fairy coins on the towpath. Panting, she reached her own front door. She dived down the hallway. Using both hands, she slid back the bolt on the cellar door.

'Pull out the plug! Go on, do it!' she ordered herself. She stretched out her hand . . .

Then she stopped. A picture had flashed into her mind. It was the VSB, curled up on the cold cellar floor, with his big toes in his ears. Pretending like mad that all the bad things in the world had gone away.

I can't do it, she decided, pulling her hand back.

She had a brief, furious argument with herself.

But you've got to do it!

I can't!

There's no other way!

There must be!

What is it then? Are you going to duel with

Dr Fell yourself? Who do you know who's as good as him with a sword?

Out of the blue, a look of hope flickered on Juniper's face. A crazy scheme had just come into her head. 'It won't work,' her brain warned her. 'You haven't thought it through. It's way, way too risky.'

But she was desperate. All she could think about was getting rid of Dr Fell without sending the VSB into oblivion too. She raced back to the kitchen and raked about in the bin.

'Found it!' She pulled out the Gladiator's vial and wiped off the macaroni cheese with a green frill.

Was there anything left in it? Or had it all leaked away? She held it up to the light and shook it. There was a sudden golden flare. A few drops of Essence of Gladiator were left in the bottom.

Was it enough? She cradled the vial in her hand so no more spilled. She carried it down the cellar steps. All the way, warning bells shrilled in her brain, but she ignored them.

Her hand shook as she poured the oil into the E-Nose. The little machine got lively immediately. It started chuntering away, spewing out tape. Juniper waited. Her breath felt locked inside her throat.

When it started to wail and shriek, she let out a long sigh, '*Phew!*' She'd thought it wasn't going to work.

Coils of tape shot out like party poppers. Green lights sparkled emerald-bright. Then, just as before, it calmed down. It had finished assembling the smell molecules.

But where was he? Juniper peered around. Away from the circle of light the cellar was pitch black. It was a warren of tunnels and secret rooms.

She sniffed. Could that be a whiff of pigeon dung? A hint of geranium-scented oil? Then, *wham*, the full flowery perfume hit her. The smell of a gladiator, greasing himself up for a fight.

'Hello?' called Juniper, timidly. 'Are you there?'

'OW!' A grunt of pain came out of the darkness.

That was the sound of a gladiator, making himself look drop-dead gorgeous for his lady fans.

# Chapter Fourteen

U p in her study, Juniper's mum had almost given up her desperate hunt. She knew she was a bit vague at times, but surely she hadn't moved those vials out of Dr Fell's cabinet? They were too precious to leave lying about.

Where else could they be? she wondered, tapping her biker boots. Puzzled, she raked a hand through her purple hair, then twisted her diamond eyebrow studs thoughtfully.

'I know!'

With a swish of her gold-fringed skirt, she dived through the titan arum leaves. She began searching a cupboard she'd forgotten about. It was the last place she could think of to look. If this failed, she was going downstairs to find Juniper.

Maybe she knows what's happened to them, she thought.

When the Gladiator first saw Juniper, he threw down his tweezers and snatched up his shield and sword.

'*Ugh?*' he enquired, lumbering to his feet.

He hadn't been brainy before. Now his thinking power was about the same as a sheep's. The E-Nose had tried its best, but it couldn't work miracles. When smell molecules get mixed up with macaroni cheese, you can't expect perfect results.

Juniper's legs were wobbling like jelly.

She thought, I've made a big mistake.

The Gladiator might smell of flowers and have a chest as smooth as a baby's bum, but he was a muscly hunk who could lop your head off with one stroke of that savage sword.

She said shakily, 'Could you come with me, please?'

'*Ugh?*' said the Gladiator. He didn't speak any English. He'd been captured in Germania by Roman legions.

Juniper could see he didn't understand

her, so she used some simple sign language. She beckoned and pointed up the cellar stairs.

She was expecting an angry roar. She got ready to run.

But he sheathed his sword! He followed her, meek as a lamb.

He wasn't furious. He wasn't even puzzled. He knew what was happening next. The cellar was exactly like the tunnels, dungeons and dressing rooms under a Roman arena. He felt quite at home here. And now that he'd made himself look dreamy, he was ready to go out and fight.

So he strode eagerly after Juniper. His fans were waiting.

That was easy, thought Juniper, astonished.

He paused under the light, took out his mirror and did a last-minute check on his hairstyle. He never wore a helmet. What was the point in being so handsome if the crowd couldn't see you?

'You look great,' said Juniper. 'Now let's go!'

She dreaded to think what was happening to Kit and the VSB. Dr Fell was as dangerous as a rattlesnake. He'd always been ruthless, but losing his nose and being banished from Court had completely turned his brain.

It was a good job no one was around. The strange pair hurrying out of 19 Canal Street would have made their eyes pop. A wild-looking child in a green party frock and scruffy white trainers. Followed by a scary Roman gladiator who smelled of geraniums.

Up in her study, Juniper's mum shook her head hopelessly. She'd given up. Dr Fell's vials seemed to have vanished off the face of the earth.

I'll go and ask Juniper, she thought.

Then she heard the front door slam. She clanged down the iron stairs. 'Juniper!'

There was no answer. She wouldn't have gone far. Perhaps just to sniff a tree by the canal. Juniper's mum opened the door.

There was no sign of her daughter. Only an empty towpath and the canal sliding past, with plastic bottles and burger boxes jostling on top.

Where is she? she wondered.

She couldn't have gone out to see friends. Because she didn't have any. Juniper's mum was pleased about that. She'd raised Juniper *her* way, without interference from anyone.

The experiment had been a great success. It had brought her lots of respect from other smell experts.

Then she peered into the distance. And started to get worried. She saw a tiny bright-green figure, flitting like a dragonfly through barbed wire and ruined buildings.

That's Juniper! she thought. Where's she going?

Was that someone plodding behind her? She couldn't see clearly, because at that moment they both disappeared into a tangle of tall purple weeds. She only saw that the other figure looked huge and hulking . . .

'*Juniper!*' she screamed, suddenly frantic for her daughter's safety.

She pounded down the towpath, heading for the place she'd seen them vanish. She fought her way through the weeds. There were crumbling factories all around. But no people, no signs of life at all. Except a crow, pecking at an old pizza box.

'I've lost her!' cried Juniper's mum, staring about in despair.

She saw something glittering by the toe of her boot. She crouched down to look at it.

'It's one of Juniper's sequins.'

There was another one over there. And another one. Moving slowly, her eyes searching the ground for tiny sparkles, she started to follow them.

At the church, Dr Fell hadn't run Kit through yet. He was taking his time. He was having too much fun taunting his prisoners. Being cruel was one of the few pleasures he had left.

'Did you imagine, my poor noddle,' he mocked the VSB, 'that I really had a fancy for your mother? Me? A man of rank and importance? Fancy a pig-scented peasant woman? Being within ten paces of her was foul enough! *Faugh!*'

Dr Fell spat and wiped his mouth in disgust. 'It is the only time I felt glad I had no nose!'

Kit knew his life was in danger, but he burst out, 'Don't talk about his mum like that!'

The VSB was trembling. But this time it wasn't fear, it was rage. Two spots of red flamed on his chalky cheeks. He loved his mum to bits. He'd never known his dad. He had died before the VSB was born, after a fire-eating trick that went wrong. But Mum looked after him really well. She made him wild lettuce soup, every day.

In a ball of fury, he hurled himself at Dr Fell. 'You demon!'

Dr Fell looked down. He seemed to have a scrawny, plucked chicken wrapped round his riding boot. It was the VSB, clinging on with both arms and legs.

Dr Fell tried to scrape him off with his sword hilt, like something nasty he'd trodden in.

The VSB wouldn't, couldn't, let go.

Dr Fell hopped about, shaking his leg. He looked like a giant crow doing the hokey-cokey. The VSB's teeth were rattling. But, desperately, he hung on.

'You should be grateful, wretch!' cried Dr Fell. 'I will take you to Court. You will live among *civilized* people. Not ignorant peasants!'

He didn't mention that the VSB would never see the light of day. Or ever again feel the sun on his face. He would be Dr Fell's prisoner. Slaving away as a spit boy in some dark, stifling kitchen – where he would sweat out buckets of Essence of Violet for Queen Elizabeth.

'Let go, you poxy knave!' rasped Dr Fell. 'You won't, eh? Well, I shall just have to end your friend's life!'

Several things happened at once. Dr Fell raised his rapier, the VSB dropped off his leg, Kit felt his heart stop and Juniper burst through the church doors with the Gladiator close behind her.

Dr Fell stopped in mid-swipe.

'You remade the Gladiator!' gasped Kit. 'Brilliant move!' He would turn Dr Fell into mincemeat!

'Gladiator?' said Dr Fell. 'Is this some performing fool from the fair?'

Kit almost said, 'No! He comes from your smell cabinet!' But he decided this wasn't the right time.

'*UGH?*' The Gladiator lumbered forward. His face was scrunched into a frown. He was obviously thinking hard. This *seemed* like an arena. There was sky above him. Someone to fight. Sand under his feet to soak up the blood. But where were his screaming fans?

He felt insulted. He was a star! Did they really expect him to fight in this downmarket dump? With such a pathetic turnout? There was nobody rich or famous here. Just three little kids. One as floppy as a skinned rabbit, who stared at him out of big, scared eyes.

And what about this opponent? He was used to fighting men with tridents. Men on chariots with spears. With some lions and crocs thrown in, to make it more of a challenge. Not one ugly little guy, who looked like a cockroach, with a silly, bendy sword. It wasn't worth messing up his hairstyle.

He roared out a few angry words in his own language. They meant, 'I refuse to fight in these conditions!'

But Dr Fell was prancing round him, parrying, thrusting. Even he looked puzzled. 'Defend yourself!' he cried. 'You craven coward!'

He'd been a bit worried when the Gladiator first marched in. He'd looked pretty powerful, with that great, square bull's head, those bunches of muscles. But it appeared he was going to be a pushover.

'Why won't he fight?' asked Kit.

The Gladiator seemed to have gone on strike. He'd stuck his sword in the ground and was resting on his shield. He even took his tweezers off his belt. He'd just spotted a stray chest hair.

'*Ow.*'

'For heaven's sake,' fumed Kit. 'Will you *stop* doing that? You're supposed to be saving us from Dr Fell!'

'Oh no,' said Juniper. 'Now he's using his earwax scoop.'

Then Juniper's mum rushed in.

She stopped, her eyes wide and alarmed, her brain struggling to take in what she was seeing. 'What's going on? Who are these people? Juniper! Are you all right?'

Instantly, the Gladiator perked up. He'd made a mistake! Here was someone worth impressing. She wore rich gold fringes and sparkling diamonds. She had purple boots – only royalty wore purple. She was so important, she even had purple hair! Was she a foreign empress or something?

The Gladiator stopped raking out his ears. He gave her his most dazzling smile and flexed his pecs.

You had to stay popular, especially with powerful people. They held your life in their hands. When they held their thumbs up, the emperor let you live. And the Gladiator wanted to live very much so that, one day, he could win his freedom and go back to his farm.

'Those who are about to die salute you!' bellowed the Gladiator in Latin, even though he expected to polish off Dr Fell in about two seconds flat. He might have to stretch it out a bit, to make it more entertaining.

But he'd made a big mistake. He'd underestimated Dr Fell. The Gladiator had brute strength, but Dr Fell was a skilled fencer. He had springy legs. And he was much, much smarter.

'Have at you!' Dr Fell dodged about. He took a froggy leap forward, and lunged.

'He's stabbed him!' cried Kit.

The Gladiator glanced down at his arm. After what seemed like ages, surprise showed on his face. He flicked off the bead of blood, as if it was no more than a gnat bite. Then he growled. He smoothed down his hair at the back. He picked up his great heavy sword. He might have to take this human cockroach seriously.

With a savage howl, the Gladiator ran at Dr Fell.

His audience scattered. 'This way!' yelled Juniper, dragging the VSB by his bony wrist. 'Up to the balcony!'

'Why – what – who?' stuttered Juniper's mum, looking stunned.

'Come on!' said Kit. Together they clattered up the wooden stairs.

From the balcony they had a bird's-eye view.

The Gladiator charged towards Dr Fell like an angry elephant. Sand sprayed up all around him. Laughing devilishly, Dr Fell skipped out of the way.

'*UGH?*' said the Gladiator, finding an empty space where his enemy should have been.

'Over here!' called Dr Fell. He would make short work of this muscle-bound simpleton. One stab, right through the heart.

The Gladiator didn't know much about tactics. He didn't fight with finesse. He was the crushing, trampling, hacking sort. But, in order to crush your opponent, you've got to catch him first.

And Dr Fell seemed to be in several places at once. He was as slippery as an eel. And, for once, he didn't have to worry about his nose falling off.

'He's running rings round the Gladiator,' said Kit hopelessly.

Dr Fell actually seemed to be enjoying himself. He was teasing the Gladiator. He danced temptingly forward, swirled his cloak like a bull fighter, then frisked backwards, as if to say, 'Come on then, you blockhead, catch me!'

The Gladiator's brain clanked into action. '*Ugh?*' He lumbered forward. Dr Fell lured him on. 'Faster, noddle! Faster!'

Dr Fell twirled his rapier. He was a really elegant fighter! He sighted along the blade. He was just about to deliver the killer thrust when – *Crash!* – a cloud of sand shot up. He'd fallen backwards over the drum of the cement mixer. His rapier flew out of his hand, high into the air.

'Duck!' said Kit.

The blade stabbed the wooden balcony and stuck there, twanging.

The Gladiator saw his chance. He thundered towards Dr Fell like a ten ton truck. There was no escape now. With one knee on his victim's throat, the Gladiator smoothed his hair, then raised his sword with a roar of triumph.

He looked up at the balcony for instructions. What happened next depended on them. Would it be thumbs up? Or thumbs down?

'No!' cried Juniper.

'What do you mean, no?' hissed Kit. 'No *mercy*!'

He was in a bloodthirsty mood. Dr Fell deserved to die. He didn't only steal smells, he stole children. He was a grave robber, an all-round baddie!

But Juniper ignored Kit. She stuck out her hand, thumb up. Then so did the VSB. Kit stared at him, astonished. 'What're you doing that for?' The VSB had suffered more than any of them at the hands of Old No-Nose. Didn't he want revenge?

Two thumbs up. Two undecided. Down in the arena, the Gladiator waited patiently for the mob to make up its mind. It didn't matter one way or the other to him. It was just part of the job.

Dr Fell, half throttled, made awful choking sounds: '*Urgle, urgle.*'

'Put your thumb up, Mum!' urged Juniper.

Juniper's mum still couldn't grasp what was

happening. But, for once, it was Juniper calling  the shots. Shakily, she raised her thumb.

Kit thought, I'm outvoted.

And, on second thoughts, he didn't want to see a blood bath. He raised his thumb too. It didn't make any difference. Three to one was what the Gladiator had been waiting for.

He'd already taken his knee off Dr Fell's throat. Just in time. Dr Fell had been turning purple.

While Dr Fell gasped and flapped about in the sand, Juniper took charge. She came down the steps into the arena. 'Keep him prisoner,' she told the Gladiator.

'*Ugh?*' said the Gladiator.

Juniper made signs. Mimed hands tied behind her back, then pointed to Dr Fell.

The Gladiator seemed to understand. He shrugged and hauled Dr Fell up by his ruff.

Why all this fuss about one little cockroach? he thought. It would have been easier to finish him off. But at least, this way, he didn't have to clean his sword.

Dr Fell gnashed his teeth. He didn't feel defeated or humbled. He was in a bigger rage than ever. His language hadn't improved. 'Unhand me, you poxy peasant!'

He kicked out at the Gladiator's ankle with his riding boot. The Gladiator shook him about like a rag doll. That quietened him down a bit.

It was all too much for the VSB. He was only seven years old. He hadn't been well lately and he wanted his mum. Plus, his belly was hollow with hunger.

He did his usual trick. He curled up, with his toes in his ears, then rocked himself for comfort.

'Where is Mother?' he was moaning. 'Where is my wild lettuce soup?'

Juniper's mum was staring at the VSB. She wasn't shell-shocked any more. Her brain seemed to be working at top speed. Soon, she was going to be asking some very awkward questions.

That was bad news. Kit was already thinking, Oh no, what are we going to tell her?

She was way behind on the plot. She'd been stuck in her study. She didn't even know the E-Nose had arrived, let alone everything else that had happened after that.

She was in for a terrible shock.

Kit gabbled the first words that came into his head. 'He's the Violet-Scented Boy. His mother's the Pig Woman. He was kidnapped from the fair.' He realized he'd left a lot out, but he thought, I'll leave it to Juniper.

It was *her* mum, after all.

Then Juniper's mum startled him. She seemed to ignore what he'd just been saying. She asked a question he wasn't expecting.

'What did that little boy say, about wanting his wild lettuce soup?'

# Chapter Fourteen

There was a weird little group straggling along the towpath. They looked like refugees from a circus. Juniper, in her bright, trashy party frock. Her mum, in carnival colours. Then the VSB, a sad, scruffy urchin in his coal-sack tunic. And, bringing up the rear, a Roman gladiator prodding a hopping-mad Elizabethan guy along with his sword.

Kit, up front with Juniper and her mum, looked like a typical, modern kid. But you'd think twice before asking him the time of day. Anyone with friends like these had to have *something* freaky about them.

'This whole story's incredible!' protested Juniper's mum.

She seemed to have forgotten, for the moment, about wild lettuce soup. The other

things Juniper was telling her were so mind-
boggling that they'd driven it right out of her head.

'So let's get this straight,' said Juniper's mum. 'You're telling me that the E-Nose can make people from their *smell* molecules? That it assembled these people. Except for him.' She nodded at Kit. 'And you met *him* on the towpath.'

Kit waited for her to say, 'Clear off! Juniper isn't allowed to mix with kids with smell prejudice.' But she didn't. Maybe, in the circumstances, it seemed like the least of her problems.

'So do I know *everything* now?' she asked Juniper.

'Did I tell you that if the E-Nose is switched off, they get blasted back into smell molecules?'

'Yes,' said Juniper's mum, her lips tightening. 'You told me that.'

'What about it only working with Dr Fell's special oil?' Kit spoke up, braver now that he hadn't been quizzed about his tree-sniffing habits.

'Oh yes,' said Juniper reluctantly. 'It's like

Kit said. The E-Nose won't make *anyone* from their smell molecules. Only the people from Dr Fell's vials.'

'Does that mean you've *tried* making other people?' said Juniper's mum, giving her daughter a sharp-eyed look.

'Er, er,' stuttered Juniper, her hand automatically reaching for the piece of polar mitten in her pocket.

She didn't want to admit that she'd tried to remake her dad. She didn't want to discuss that at all. It was still too painful. You don't see a dream destroyed and just get over it.

Kit could see she was struggling. He came to her help.

'Yes! We tried making another ME!' he said. 'With a piece of my sweaty T-shirt. But, like Juniper said, it just wouldn't work.'

'Hummm,' said Juniper's mum.

She sensed Juniper was keeping something from her. Sharing a secret with someone else. Her daughter shouldn't be doing that. But today she'd broken *all* the rules –

*Phew!* thought Kit. He felt sure she'd ask loads more questions, but Juniper's mum had gone quiet. She seemed to be thinking.

Kit was having a few thoughts himself. One was, Pity it only works with Dr Fell's special oil.

He could have cloned a whole army of himself. And taken over the world!

And another was, I just talked about my own sweaty smell. And I didn't get paranoid.

In its way, that was a bigger miracle than anything that had happened today.

'They all still there?' asked Kit anxiously.

He'd half turned round to check on the stragglers when Juniper said, 'Yes.' She didn't need to see them. She could smell them. The Gladiator with his flowery pong, Dr Fell, who reeked of graveyards, and the VSB, whose violet perfume was getting fainter all the time.

Kit didn't like the look of the VSB. He didn't seem so weak and floppy – he was actually keeping up – but he was crying big tears that splashed on the towpath.

'Where is Mother?' he was moaning. 'Where is my wild lettuce soup?'

'He's going on about his mum again,' Kit told Juniper. 'Poor little kid. I'm going back to cheer him up.'

'About this special oil –' began Juniper's mum, after Kit had rushed off.

'Don't even *think* about it, Mum,' said Juniper. 'You could never make it. I already asked him about it. It's got really weird ingredients. Then there're the spells.'

Juniper's mum raised her eyebrows. 'Spells?'

She turned back to look at Dr Fell. He was stomping along, squirming with fury, prodded by the Gladiator's sword. She could just about cope with the science. Theoretically, it *might* be possible to reassemble people from their smell molecules. But spells? Magic potions? That was going too far.

The Gladiator saw her glancing in his direction. His feeble brain, even more befuddled by macaroni cheese, finally came up with one single thought. *Was he looking his best?* His body, greasy with scented oils, glittered in the sun. His blond hair, dyed with pigeon dung, stuck up in stiff spikes. He flashed Juniper's mum his smouldering smile. The one that made Roman ladies' knees tremble.

For heaven's sake, thought Juniper's mum, that muscleman's an idiot! He's unbelievable!

And Dr Fell was a mad old grotbag. Hardly

the dashing rogue she'd imagined. Was someone trying to make a monkey out of her?

Suddenly she had a brainwave. She almost laughed out loud with relief. It explained everything! Why hadn't she thought of it before?

She stared around her. 'Come clean, Juniper. Where are the cameras?'

'What are you *talking* about?'

'We're on one of those telly programmes, aren't we? That set people up!'

'No, we're not,' said Juniper.

'We must be! It's the *only* explanation.'

'Why don't you listen to me?' said Juniper hotly. 'You're always *telling* me stuff. About how other kids are stupid because they've got smell prejudice. And how I should keep away from them because they'll mess up my mind. But Kit's not like that!'

'OK, OK,' said Juniper's mum hastily. 'Just calm down.' A little thought wriggled at the back of her brain. Could it be Juniper isn't happy?

No, she reassured herself. She would have told me.

But there were lots of things lately that

Juniper hadn't told her mum. Including how she saw her future – in frozen Arctic wastes, where no one would call her 'freak'.

'Look, I believe you!' said Juniper's mum. 'I believe *everything* you've just said.'

'No, you don't,' said Juniper, still looking grim and angry. 'But you will in a minute. Soon as we get home, I'll get the E-Nose to assemble another person. Then you can see for yourself.'

'Wait a second,' said Juniper's mum. 'I thought you said it only worked with the smells from Dr Fell's vials? And you've used them all up.'

But Juniper had already burst through the door of 19 Canal Street and was on her way down to the cellar. She was so eager to reach the E-Nose that she didn't notice two red eyes, glinting in the shadows. It was the black rat, watching her.

As she followed her daughter, Juniper's mum checked the vials off on her fingers.

'Essence of Gladiator, Essence of Monster, Essence of Myself. That's three used up. Hang on, what happened to Pig Woman?'

# Chapter Fifteen

Kit was dragging behind with the VSB. He longed to make him smile, but he didn't know how to do it.

'How would you feel,' Kit asked himself, 'if you were a Violet-Scented Elizabethan Monster stuck in the twenty-first century? Without your mum?'

At least Dr Fell couldn't harm him now. But the VSB kept throwing scared, furtive looks back over his shoulder. He seemed to think that Dr Fell was still dangerous.

He was right. Dr Fell would never surrender. The same old passion still burned inside him – getting into Queen Elizabeth's good books. To do that he had to continue his nose quest. And get his hands on his Monster again. The VSB was his one-way ticket back to London. How dare this gang of noddles try to nab him?

But he was one hundred per cent certain he would get him back. He wasn't downhearted. This was just a small blip in his plans!

His crazy brain conjured up a picture. It was Queen Elizabeth, touching him lightly on the shoulder with a sword and saying, 'Arise, Sir Thomas Fell!'

'Have a care, clodpate!' he raged, as the Gladiator's massive sandal mashed his toes.

'*Ugh?*' said the Gladiator, stepping closer and accidentally crushing Dr Fell's other foot.

Kit tried to take the VSB's mind off his mother and wild lettuce soup.

'I thought you hated that Dr Fell,' he said.

The VSB scrunched his monkey face into a fierce scowl. 'I do hate him, sir! He is a fiend. He has done many foul deeds.'

'So why did you vote for him to live? You know, back there in the arena? I mean, I was dead surprised.'

The VSB looked puzzled for a few seconds. As if he'd been surprised too. Then he finally said, 'When he came to the fair, he made Mother feel like a fine lady.'

'Oh,' said Kit. It didn't seem like a very good reason to him, for saving someone who'd stolen you from your family. Then kept you prisoner, just because they wanted your sweat.

But they'd reached the door of 19 Canal Street. Kit turned round and waited for Dr Fell and the Gladiator. The Gladiator had stopped to admire his reflection in a puddle.

Problems Kit had hardly considered were beginning to scare him. They seemed mind-boggling, too big for his brain to cope with. What do you do with three reassembled people from the past? Keep them here, in the twenty-first century, where they didn't belong? Or switch off the E-Nose and obliterate them?

Getting rid of Dr Fell didn't bother him. He'd be cheering and yelling, 'Good riddance!' But he didn't want the VSB to be blasted back to smell molecules. And what about the Gladiator? He was vain and he'd never win *Mastermind*, but Kit thought, I can't help it. I like the guy!

He was having wild thoughts: the Gladiator could be my minder. He could come with me everywhere. He could sleep at home in the spare bed.

He could see it now. Some loudmouth would yell, 'You smell!' Then his minder would come clumping up, looking like King Kong after a full body shave.

'Care to say that again?' Kit would ask casually.

But it could cause trouble at home. For a start, you'd never get in the bathroom. The Gladiator would *always* be in there, tweezing, dyeing his hair with pigeon dung, pinching Mum's favourite perfume ...

'Kit, come down here, quick!' It was Juniper's voice.

Kit shook off his daydreams. 'This way!' he said to the VSB. 'Down to the cellar!'

The Gladiator hustled Dr Fell in through the front door. And then a dreadful thing happened. There was a mirror in the hallway. Naturally, the Gladiator turned to inspect himself in it. Was that a pimple that needed popping?

Dr Fell didn't need a second chance. He wrapped his black cloak tightly round him and tiptoed up the iron stairs, fast as a ferret. He didn't even make a clang.

'*UGH?*' said the Gladiator, finally tearing

himself away from the mirror. Where had the cockroach gone? He hadn't seen him escape!

The Gladiator let out a furious bellow. His brain began wrestling with the problem. The cockroach either went *up* the stairs. Or *down* the stairs. The Gladiator made the wrong choice and went to look for him in the cellar.

On the top floor of the ex-cat-food factory, Dr Fell flung back his head. He gave his maniac's laugh. He was free! If only he had his rapier. First he must find a weapon. Then settle some scores.

'Those thieves will be sorry they sought to steal my Monster! And snatch the prize for violet perfume from under my very nose! I will kill them all. All!'

Cackling horribly, he opened the door to Juniper's mum's study.

He dodged under the titan arum leaves. He didn't notice the bud, just above his head, ripening in the sunshine from the long windows.

He leapt back. 'What wizardry is this?' The computer hummed at him. Bright, swirly patterns spun like tiny tornadoes across its screen.

But he was too crazy to be scared. Nothing

would stop him getting what he wanted. Not all the wizards, all the sorcerers, in the world.

Then he spotted something else. 'My smell cabinet!'

He slid out the bottom tray. They weren't the human noses he craved. You couldn't smell with them. They kept falling off. But they were better than nothing.

'But wait!' said Dr Fell. He held up a black, shrivelled object. 'Fortune is smiling on me!'

He thought he'd run out of human noses. This one was a bit past its sell-by date. But Dr Fell's mad brain didn't mind that.

He opened the glue pot. Then fumbled about under the black silk hanky. When he whisked it off, the prune from Juniper's mum's muesli was stuck firmly to his face.

He stuffed the other noses in his pouch, as spares.

Dr Fell sprang back down the stairs. He hadn't found a weapon yet. First he would arm himself. Then those poxy peasants had better say their prayers.

Down in the cellar, Juniper asked Kit, 'You've got the Essence of Pig Woman, haven't you?'

'Have I?' said Kit. He'd forgotten all about it. He searched in his pocket. *Phew*, the vial wasn't broken. He handed it over.

'What do you want it for?' he asked her.

Juniper didn't answer. She was stooping over the E-Nose. Its little lights made her face glow eerie green.

'Don't tell me,' gasped Kit. His stomach felt full of wild, beating wings. 'You're not going to bring *her* back!'

'Mum doesn't believe me,' said Juniper stubbornly. 'So I'm going to give her a little demonstration.'

Kit stared hard at Juniper's mum. Surely she was going to put her foot down! Say, 'This isn't a good idea.' Hadn't these reassembled people caused enough trouble already?

But Juniper's mum was strangely silent. She looked at the VSB, collapsed in a sad little heap on the floor. All that walking had worn him out. He didn't even have the strength to ask for Mother or wild lettuce soup. Soon he would curl up hedgehog tight, plug his toes in his ears to shut out the scary world and fall asleep.

Poor kid, she was thinking. His own mother

had used him shamelessly. She'd made into a freak. She'd put him on show and was poisoning him into the bargain!

This isn't going to work, she thought as Juniper tipped the golden oil into the E-Nose. But, in a way, she wished it would. She had a few words to say to that Pig Woman.

The E-Nose started its merry chattering. Tape came out, covered with squiggles.

Juniper's mum tapped her purple boot impatiently. 'But that's what it's *supposed* to do. Look, it's just writing out the smell recipe.'

She was beginning to get very angry. What was Juniper up to? She'd wasted all those precious smells from the past.

'You'd better have kept all the recipes,' said Juniper's mum. 'I need those for my scratch-and-sniff book.'

'What?' said Juniper, without looking round.

She and Kit were concentrating fiercely. Waiting for the E-Nose to move on to the next stage. Despite herself, Juniper's mum couldn't help staring at it too. The nail-biting tension was catching.

The VSB copied them. He gazed, wide-eyed, at the glowing machine. But he didn't  have a clue what was going on.

Kit wanted to tell him, 'You're going to see your mum in a minute.' That should put a smile on his face. But he thought he'd better not give the VSB the good news just yet. What if something went wrong?

None of them noticed the Gladiator padding down the cellar stairs in his sandals. He didn't pay any attention to them. He strode off into the darkness, poking his sword into all the cellar's dark corners. He was looking for the cockroach.

Dr Fell was in the kitchen, opening drawers. He pulled out some nutcrackers and an egg whisk.

Humm, what are these, he wondered. Instruments of torture?

He stuffed them into his belt. They might come in handy later.

There were many fine sharp knives. He stuck a selection of these in his belt, then pulled a meat skewer out of the cupboard. It wasn't as good as a rapier, but it could make a nasty hole in someone. Armed to the teeth

with kitchen implements, he crept to the top of
the cellar steps.

Juniper's mum stared in disbelief at the
E-Nose. The little machine seemed to be
driven by demons! It jumped about on the
barrel and howled like a banshee, while its
lights flashed on and off in a frenzy.

'What's the matter with it?'

'It's making the Pig Woman,' said Juniper
coolly.

'You *are* kidding me, aren't you?' Juniper's
mum almost begged.

Then a foul stench filled the cellar.

'Pig manure!' pronounced Juniper.

But you didn't have to have her super-
sensitive nose. You couldn't help smelling it. It
swamped the Gladiator's flowery scent and
even the fishy pong of cat food. The VSB's
fading violet perfume didn't stand a chance.

'*Phew!*' said Kit. 'What a stink!' It brought
tears to his eyes.

But the VSB perked up. His dull eyes got
brighter. He wrinkled his nose. He knew that
smell.

'Mother!' he cried.

A high-pitched squealing sound came from  somewhere. *Eeee, eeee, eeee!*

A slippery pink piglet shot out of the darkness and raced across the cellar. It was moving so fast its tiny, twinkling trotters were just a blur.

Its smell molecules had somehow found their way into the Pig Woman's essence. That's no surprise, when a person likes to relax by sitting in the pigpen, smoking a clay pipe and giving her piglets a cuddle.

The piglet disappeared into the depths of the cellar. It bounced off something big. *Eeee, eeee, eeee!*

'*Ugh?*' came a confused grunt. It was the Gladiator. Still searching for his prisoner.

For a brief moment, there was silence in the cellar.

'Mother?' came the VSB's quavery voice again. His eyes, which had been bright with hope a few seconds ago, were darkening with despair.

But then came a roaring voice, loud enough to call back her pigs when they were rootling for acorns in distant woods.

'My Violet-Scented Boy!'

Like a juggernaut, the Pig Woman came crashing out of the shadows. She was gigantically fat, she was smelly, she was smeared with pig poo. But she had a warm and generous heart. And she loved the VSB more then anything. She lifted him up in strong, muscly arms.

'I have searched high and low for you.'

The VSB hugged her like a clingy little octopus, as if he never wanted to let her go.

Kit's eyes were prickling with tears again. But for different reasons. This meeting between mother and son was really touching. '*Awwwww!*' he said.

Juniper was wiping her eyes too.

Juniper's mum was hit by a whirlwind of different feelings. 'Is this really happening?' she marvelled.

She watched the Pig Woman give the VSB a big bear hug, with tears sliding down her grimy face. 'My son, my son!'

Juniper's mum frowned. 'That doesn't look like the kind of woman who would deliberately poison her son with wild lettuce,' she told herself. 'Perhaps she didn't know what she was doing.'

But there was no time to wonder about that. Because, at that moment, a black, spidery leg hooked round the cellar door. A shrivelled prune nose poked out after it. It was Dr Fell, coming to take back his Monster.

'He stole me from you, Mother!' cried the VSB, hiding his face in her greasy smock.

The Pig Woman bellowed with rage.

'Oh no,' muttered Dr Fell, 'not that plaguey woman again.'

He skipped lightly down the steps, flourishing his meat skewer. Kitchen knives bristled in his belt. She was really getting on his nerves. He'd just put her top of his list of people he was going to run through.

The Pig Woman shook her huge, ham-sized fist at him. 'You stole my boy! What a fool I was! I thought you a fine gentleman!'

She plonked the VSB behind her out of harm's way. Then got ready to charge.

Dr Fell's eyes glittered madly. He knew she had just minutes to live. The Pig Woman was good at brawling. At the fair she often challenged men to wrestling matches. She always overpowered them. She was so greasy that they couldn't get a grip.

But Dr Fell was a Master Swordsman. He'd out-fenced the most famous fighters in Europe. Even when he lost his nose, he'd gone on to win the duel with a deadly rapier thrust.

'*Ugh?*'

Dr Fell looked round.

It was the Gladiator. He'd given up searching for his prisoner in the dark nooks and crannies of the cellar. After a few seconds spent plucking out his nose hair, he'd come stomping out into the light.

Dr Fell grinned a wolfish grin. Two noddles for him to dispatch. Even better. He gave his prune nose a tug, to make sure it was firmly fixed on. 'Say your prayers, peasants!'

Kit, Juniper and Juniper's mum looked helplessly on. What's going to happen now! thought Kit.

The VSB couldn't bear to watch. He rolled into a dark corner and stayed there, curled up tight with his toes in his ears.

'Stop it!' shouted Juniper. 'You're scaring the VSB!'

But the reassembled grown-ups ignored her. They were hell-bent on violence. They were completely out of control!

With a savage war cry, the Gladiator thudded towards Dr Fell. The Pig Woman wasn't far behind.

The floor shook. Was Dr Fell going to end up flat? As if two steam rollers had squashed him? But the old fox wasn't even there. He'd skipped nimbly out of their way.

The Pig Woman skidded to a stop, but with a shuddering crash the Gladiator collided with the cellar wall.

'*Doh!*' said the Gladiator, rubbing his forehead. He blundered groggily about. Where was that cockroach now?

The Gladiator was temporarily out of action. But the Pig Woman didn't hesitate. She launched an attack on her own. She came pounding towards Dr Fell, both arms outstretched, to grab him in her favourite wrestling hold. She could squeeze the breath out of a man's body that way.

Her pigpen breath hit him first. That was enough to poleaxe most people. But it didn't affect Old No-Nose. He just stepped casually to one side before the rest of her arrived.

The Gladiator came swaying up. He was

still seeing stars. He hacked at Dr Fell with his great iron sword.

'*UGH?*' Dr Fell wasn't there.

'Enough of this nonsense,' Dr Fell decided, from over by the cellar steps. 'Just run them through.' It wasn't any fun, fighting two such clumsy fools.

'Prepare to die!' he cried to the Pig Woman. She was taking as long to turn round as an ocean liner. But he pirouetted on the spot, his black cloak swirling.

His meat skewer stabbed the air, in a few practice thrusts. Then he moved in for the real thing.

At last, Juniper's mum's stunned brain sparked into life. 'Stop him!' it screamed at her. 'There's going to be a massacre!' After the Pig Woman and the Gladiator, they would be next.

She ran towards the E-Nose.

'No!' said Kit and Juniper together. Standing shoulder to shoulder, they blocked her way.

'Don't be stupid!' shrieked Juniper's mum, trying to force her way between them. 'We've got to switch it off!'

She was too late to save the Pig Woman. Dr Fell was already lunging at her heart.

But a millisecond before he struck, the black rat bit through the electric cable. Instantly, the lights on the E-Nose failed.

*Fizzz!* Dr Fell, the Gladiator and the Pig Woman exploded in a shower of stars. Their smell molecules mingled together, then drifted to the floor like a spent firework.

They'd all been blasted into thin air but, for a few seconds, Kit couldn't believe they'd really gone.

'The VSB!' said Juniper.

Hoping against hope, they both raced to the dark corner where he'd hidden himself.

At first Kit thought he could see him, snuggled up into a ball. But when Juniper cried, in a heartbroken voice, 'He's gone too,' he knew it was only his mind playing cruel tricks.

The VSB's last smell molecule lingered in the air for a moment, like a tiny twinkling light, then went out.

# Chapter Sixteen

F or a few seconds, a cocktail of scents
hung in the air – pig poo, mouldy
graveyards, geraniums. And so faint that only
Juniper's superior smelling skills could detect it
– a hint of violets.

Dr Fell's specially preserved human smells
had all been used up. The E-Nose had no
power any more. It was just a grey metal box.

'It's over,' whispered Juniper.

Did she sound wistful? For a few hours, the
big empty spaces in the old factory had been
filled with people. Number 19 Canal Street
had buzzed with noise, colour and different
smells. It had been scary. But also the most
exciting day of her life.

Now they'd all gone. Even the piglet. The
cellar was quiet again. Except for the usual

melancholy sounds: the *drip, drip, drip* of canal
water on stone, the sad *plops* of frogs or toads
in faraway corners.

None of them heard the scurrying of tiny
feet. It was the black rat. His hair had stopped
standing on end like a loo brush.

'Get out of here,' his ratty brain told him.

He didn't want to stay in a place where
snacks gave you electric shocks. He was going
back to seafaring. Riding the waves on a
burger box was much less dangerous.

He slipped out – through the iron grille and
on to the canal bank.

Juniper's mum seemed to be speaking in a
dream.

'I'm sure she didn't know she was poisoning
him.'

'What?' Kit stopped staring at the place
where the VSB had disappeared. His head
snapped round. 'What did you just say?'

Juniper's startled voice echoed his own.
'Mum, what do you mean? Who was
poisoning who?'

Juniper's mum gave a sigh. She thought,
Why did you open your big mouth?

She should have kept all this secret. It was

really going to upset them. But it was too late now.

She took a deep breath. 'I know why the VSB smelled like he did. And I know why he was so sick. It was that wild lettuce soup his mother kept feeding him. It makes you smell of violets, but it poisons you at the same time.'

'He liked it!' protested Kit. 'He was always going on about it – "Where is my wild lettuce soup?"'

'Yes, but he never knew it was making him sick. And neither did she. Why should she? She was an Elizabethan Pig Woman! I'm a twenty-first-century scientist and even I didn't know what wild lettuce does.'

'So that's why he got stronger after Dr Fell stole him away,' said Kit.

Juniper's mum nodded. 'It sounds weird to say it but by kidnapping him, Dr Fell did him a big favour.'

'Oh, great choice!' said Kit. 'Either he gets slowly poisoned by his mum, or kept as a prisoner by Dr Fell.'

'Maybe it wasn't like that at all,' said Juniper's mum. 'Maybe he lived a long, happy life.'

'Come on!' said Kit. He knew she was only trying to cheer him up. 'Can't we find out what *did* happen to him?' Kit begged her. 'From history books?'

But he knew there was probably no chance. The VSB wasn't a famous person. He was just some poor little fairground freak.

Juniper's mum said, 'He might be mentioned somewhere. I'll search the historical records.' But she didn't sound hopeful.

Juniper had been very quiet. Now she chipped in, 'She didn't know wild lettuce was poisonous. I'm sure she didn't. But did she know it makes you smell of violets? Did she *deliberately* make her own kid into a freak?'

'So what if she did?' said Kit. 'It made them some extra money. And he was proud when people came to sniff him. He *liked* being a freak.'

'Well, I don't,' said Juniper.

You could have heard a pin drop in the cellar. Even the sad *plops* of frogs were silent.

'What do you mean?' said Juniper's mum, sounding hurt and puzzled.

Alarm bells were clanging in Kit's brain. *Whoops!* he thought. Family row!

Words rushed out of Juniper's mouth like a dam bursting: 'You made *me* into a freak. Just like the VSB. Only I sniff trees and other kids' armpits! And now I've got no friends. And I've got to go and live at the North Pole!'

'Don't be ridiculous!' said Juniper's mum. 'I was only trying to protect you from people with smell prejudice. It was for your own good.'

But for once her voice was shaky with doubt. And Kit knew why. The words came out of his mouth before he could stop them.

'It wasn't for her own good. It was for *your* smell research. It said so on your computer.'

Juniper's mum was furious. She whirled round. 'What were you doing looking at my computer? At my private notes? How *dare* you? Get out of my house this instant!'

'Don't talk to my friend like that!' yelled Juniper.

'I thought you said you didn't *have* any friends!'

Kit squirmed uncomfortably. But he didn't leave. Juniper needed someone on her side.

'I don't know why you're so mad at me!' yelled Juniper's mum at her daughter. 'You're the one that wasted all my human smells! What on earth did you think you were doing?'

'I was trying to bring Dad back,' said Juniper desperately.

There was another terrible silence. No one shouted.

*Drip, drip, drip,* went the canal water down the cellar walls.

All at once, Juniper's face crumpled into tears.

'Come here,' said her mum. Juniper rushed forward. They wrapped their arms round each other in a big bear hug.

*Awwww,* thought Kit.

He suddenly changed his mind about going. He thought, Better leave them to it.

They had important things to sort out.

He tiptoed up the cellar steps. He could hear their voices behind him. They weren't shouting any more. They were talking quietly, but he couldn't hear what they were saying.

Kit closed the front door of 19 Canal Street softly behind him.

He walked home in a trance. It was rush hour. Buses roared past him. People pushed him out of their way. But he didn't notice. He didn't listen out for those mocking voices, '*Phew*, you pong!' Or fret that he hadn't sprayed himself with Gladiator for seven whole hours.

He didn't even worry that he was late home and his mum was going to have a fit.

Instead, he was thinking about *them* – Dr Fell, the Gladiator, the Pig Woman and, of course, the VSB. He couldn't get them out of his mind. They'd seemed so real. It was hard to believe they'd dissolved into starry mist.

*Parp!* A horn blast almost burst his eardrums. He teetered on the kerb. He'd been about to step under a bus!

'You nearly got yourself killed!' he told himself, shaking with shock. 'Face up to it! You're *never* going to see them again. You're *never* going to know how their lives turned out.'

He didn't *want* to know about the VSB anyway. It was bound to be tragic.

'Just forget about him. Right?' he ordered himself sternly.

# Chapter Seventeen

T wo days later, Kit was back in the kitchen of 19 Canal Street.

He'd been wandering along the towpath. 'I'm not going anywhere near that crazy cat-food factory!' he'd told himself. But somehow he'd found his feet heading in that direction.

'Hey!' Juniper had yelled, out of one of the tall windows. 'I've been looking for you. Come to a party!'

'Mum's celebrating,' explained Juniper, opening the door for Kit, 'because she's finished *The Wonderful World of Smells*. It's going to be published next year by Hamster Children's Books.'

'*Hamster* Children's Books?' said Kit scornfully. 'That's just too cuddly! They should call themselves Killer Shark Children's Books. Kids would think that was cool.'

'Did you know . . .' began Juniper.

Oh no, thought Kit. Here comes one of her fascinating facts about smells.

'. . . that somewhere in Australia the sea was crowded with swimmers. Hundreds of them. All splashing about. And this poor kid had picked a scab off his knee. And from a mile out at sea a shark smelled his blood, and it came speeding in and knocked all the other swimmers out of the way to get to him?'

Kit wasn't listening. He was having second thoughts.

'On the other hand,' he was arguing with himself, 'hamsters aren't always cute.'

He was thinking about his little sister's pet hamster. It had long, yellow teeth and a terrible temper. Its biggest thrill was biting children. It would hide in its straw thinking, Come on, kid, make my day. Try sticking your finger through the bars.

Juniper said suddenly, 'Mum says, can I go with you to places?'

'What?' said Kit, startled. 'What do you mean, *places*?'

'Places where kids go. Like the shopping  mall and the skatepark. Maybe to the cinema.'

Kit felt torn in two directions. He knew he'd promised to teach her to mix with *normal* kids, but he'd only just stopped worrying about his smell. What would happen when he had her tagging along, sniffing trees, smelling armpits, asking boys if they could wee on the soles of their feet like bush babies? He'd have a whole new set of problems.

'Nightmare!' Kit sighed to himself.

'Cos Mum and me, we did a lot of talking,' said Juniper eagerly. 'And now, I don't want to go and live at the North Pole any more.'

'Oh . . . good,' said Kit, nodding slowly. He didn't ask what they'd talked about. That was their private business. But it seemed like they'd sorted out a few problems.

'So where are we going then?' asked Juniper.

'Er, er,' said Kit, trying frantically to think of somewhere his friends wouldn't be seen dead.

'There's this church hall where my Gran goes,' he started saying. 'It's mostly old wrinklies, but kids can come along too! You can have a cup of tea and a biscuit. You can play –'

\*

'Bingo!' shouted Juniper's mum, up in her study.

She'd just made a brilliant discovery. She should be getting ready for the party but, in the past two days, when she and Juniper hadn't been having heart to hearts, she'd spent hours trying to find out what had happened to the VSB.

At first she'd had no luck at all. There wasn't a single mention of him anywhere. She'd almost given up. But moments ago she'd been surfing the Net and come up with something spectacular.

It was on the screen now. She hit a button and printed it out. *Whirr.* Then snatched up the pages and leapt from her chair.

The titan arum leaves reached out to grab her. She dodged aside. How much bigger could that bud get? It had seemed on the point of bursting ages ago. But the foulest-smelling plant in the world wasn't going to flower until it was good and ready.

Juniper's mum went clattering down the iron stairs. Her eyebrow studs sparkled. She had an orange and red skirt on today. It clashed terribly with her purple biker boots, but it swirled around her like dancing flames.

As she exploded into the kitchen, Kit was  just saying, 'And you can even get your corns done.'

And Juniper was asking, suspiciously, 'Are you *sure* that's where the cool kids hang out?'

'Look at this!' said Juniper's mum, thrusting the printed-out pages into Kit's hand.

Kit stared at them. He screwed up his eyes. He stared at them again. 'What's it say? Is it a poem or something? I can't make sense of it,' he said.

Juniper's mum snatched the pages back. 'It's an Elizabethan ballad,' she said, 'about the VSB.'

'You're kidding me!' said Kit.

He'd thought about the VSB a lot in the last couple of days. He'd tried not to, but he just couldn't get him out of his mind. Even Juniper, who'd been busy persuading Mum to let her have a life of her own, had seen him, curled-up, in her dreams.

'But the point is,' said Juniper's mum, 'this ballad is about him when he was grown up. He didn't die young of wild-lettuce poisoning.'

'So he was Dr Fell's prisoner for the rest of

his life?' asked Kit wildly. 'Just don't tell me any more. I can't stand it!'

Juniper's mum shook her head. 'That didn't happen either,' she said.

'Then tell us what did happen,' begged Juniper.

'I should have found it before,' Juniper's mum started saying. 'I just never thought of looking at Elizabethan ballads, but they were very popular back then. They wrote songs about lots of famous people.'

'Did the VSB get famous?' interrupted Kit, goggle-eyed. 'I can't believe it!'

'Oh yes,' said Juniper's mum. 'And very rich too.'

'Are you *sure* this ballad's about him?' asked Juniper.

'Listen to this,' said Juniper's mum. She read out the first verse.

*Masters, friends, good people draw near.*
*I sing of a curious fellow,*
*Who, when he takes his rest,*
*Curls up like a squirrel in his nest*
*And crams a toe into each ear,*
*As snug as a bung in a barrel of beer!*

'It's got to be him!' said Kit, happily. 'It  couldn't be anyone else! So how did he get away from Dr Fell?'

'Hummm.' Juniper's mum puzzled over the verses. 'I'm not an Elizabethan expert. Some of this is quite hard to understand.'

'Just *try*,' begged Juniper.

'Well, here goes. It seems that Dr Fell put Queen Elizabeth into a bad mood.'

'Did his nose fall off again?' asked Kit.

'Not this time,' said Juniper's mum. 'Maybe he found some extra-strong glue. No, what happened was quite simple. He presented a bottle of the VSB's sweat to Queen Elizabeth. He made a big song and dance about it. Said it was the finest Violet Essence in the whole world. Swore it was his own secret recipe – that he'd slaved away night and day to make it.'

Kit could just imagine it. Dr Fell in his best gold nose. With his springy legs and black cloak swirling around him, bowing and scraping to Her Majesty. While all the courtiers sniggered.

'He begged her to open the bottle,' continued Juniper's mum. 'He said, "Your Majesty! I promise that this violet perfume will make you swoon with pleasure!" So she took a big sniff.'

'And all she smelled was . . . sweat!' said Juniper.

'Exactly,' said her mum. 'The VSB hadn't eaten wild lettuce soup for weeks. His violet smell was completely gone, but because Dr Fell had no nose, he didn't know that.'

'So did she chop off his head?' asked Kit eagerly. He was a bit hazy about Queen Elizabeth, but he knew that if you annoyed her, you didn't keep your head for long.

'She was going to,' said Juniper's mum. 'She said, "Is this some kind of *jest*?" Anyway, when she'd calmed down a bit, she banished him to the Low Countries.'

'So what happened after that?' asked Kit. Strangely, he felt quite glad that Dr Fell hadn't ended up headless. Being noseless was bad enough.

Juniper's mum shrugged. She flicked through the ballad's fifty-six verses.

'It doesn't say. This is about the VSB's life. Not Dr Fell's. But what it *does* say is, after Dr Fell left in a hurry, they found the VSB. Still locked in his house.'

'Was the VSB all right?' asked Juniper  anxiously.

'It says he was as fat and rosy as a piglet.'

*'Fat and rosy?'* marvelled Kit. It was hard to imagine. He'd only ever seen the VSB looking like a Twiglet. With a skin as white as fungus.

'Well,' said Juniper's mum, 'I suppose he wasn't being poisoned any more. And it didn't make sense for Dr Fell to starve him. He wanted him fit and healthy. Anyway, the VSB was rescued. He got presented at Court. And it says that Queen Elizabeth showed "much mirth at his tumbling tricks".'

'Is that all the ballad says then?' asked Kit. 'That he became Queen Elizabeth's favourite and got rich and famous?'

'Not quite,' said Juniper's mum, checking the last verses. 'It says that he sent for his mother. She lived at Court and shared his good fortune.'

'The Pig Woman at Court!' said Kit. 'I hope she had a good scrub before she went!'

'It says here she became a fine lady,' said Juniper's mum, raising her eyebrows.

She could hardly believe it either.

But the VSB's mum took to being posh like

a pig to a muddy puddle. Soon she was wearing silk and jewels and ordering her servants about. She had more airs and graces than a duchess. She had bigger ruffs than Queen Elizabeth! She always knew she should have been born rich.

'But didn't she start cooking the VSB wild lettuce soup?' asked Juniper. 'And making him sick again?'

'Shouldn't think so,' said Juniper's mum. 'That was poor people's food. I expect when they got rich they only ate posh nosh. But anyway, she can't have done. Because it says here the VSB lived to be eighty-three.'

'That's just brilliant!' said Kit.

He felt his face crack into an enormous grin. He'd taken it for granted that the VSB's life was tragic. Knowing it wasn't had shifted a big weight off his shoulders. 'Now I won't worry about him any more,' said Kit.

'But what about the Gladiator?' asked Juniper. 'Can't you find out about him?'

'Come on!' said her mum. 'You can't expect miracles. I'm amazed we found out about the VSB. The Gladiator lived back in Roman times. And we didn't even know his name.'

Juniper nodded sadly. They would never  find out.

But Dr Fell could have told her. It was carved on the Gladiator's stone coffin when Dr Fell smashed it open.

'Here lies a Gladiator of Rome, who fell in the arena.'

The Gladiator had fought many battles. He'd always hoped to win his freedom. But it never happened. Then one day he got beaten by somebody younger and better looking. And the Roman ladies didn't turn their thumbs up, but down instead. Only two fans came to his funeral. He was buried in his gladiator's costume with his weapons by his side.

Juniper's mum was looking at her watch. 'Is it that time already? Come on, you two, grab those trays of sausage rolls.'

Half an hour later, Kit whispered, 'I've been to wilder school assemblies than this.'

Only three people had turned up. The lady from the cheese counter at the Co-op, the man from the fruit stall at the market and the lifeguard from the pool where Juniper's mum went swimming. They all looked a bit lost, as if they were thinking, Why am I here?

Every day, Juniper's mum e-mailed smell experts all over the world, but she didn't know many people from her own neighbourhood. And she'd arranged this party at very short notice, for Juniper's sake.

'Juniper's right,' she'd decided. 'It's no use trying to protect her from smell-prejudiced people. She's got to learn to mix with them.'

Juniper stood nervously with Kit in a corner. She was determined to be on her best behaviour. She knew what job each person did, just by nose detection. The lifeguard smelled of chlorine and damp towels. The fruit-stall man smelled of strawberries. And the cheese-counter lady? Juniper wrinkled her nose. This was a challenge!

Without thinking, she dashed forward. 'Is that Gorgonzola you smell of? Or cheesy socks?'

There was only one way to make sure. She flung herself down on the floor. And sniffed like a dog around the lady's shoes.

Kit cringed. Oh no! Juniper had got it wrong again! He rushed up to rescue her. 'She doesn't mean to be rude. Honest,' he stammered. 'She actually *likes* smelly people.'

The cheese-counter lady opened her mouth  in outrage. 'I've never been so *insulted* –'

But before she could finish her sentence, a smell wafted from upstairs.

Up in Juniper's mum's study, the titan arum bud had finally burst. The flower was sinister. A great white lily, a metre tall, with a fat purple tongue lolling out the middle of it.

The smell was indescribable. Think of a big pile of chicken guts, left out in the blazing sun. Think of blocked toilets on a packed train from Aberdeen to Penzance. Think of Kit's egg sandwich when, after six weeks, his mum lifted the lid of his lunch box. The titan arum smelled much, much worse than all of these put together.

*Buzzz!*

A bluebottle fly dive-bombed through an open window. Followed by another and another.

Downstairs, the guests clutched their throats.

'What is that disgusting –?'

*Crash.* The hunky lifeguard was the first to faint. Then the fruit-stall man. Then the cheese-counter lady, who was more used to pongs. But even she couldn't stand it.

Kit raced outside. For ages, he staggered about, with stinging eyes, gasping for air. Then he straightened up. He took a great, deep lungful of the reeking fumes coming off the canal.

'*Ahhh*,' he said. 'That's better.'

Inside, Juniper's mum stepped over the unconscious lifeguard. 'Wimp,' she said. And to think she'd almost asked him out on a date.

She turned to Juniper, the only other person in the room who hadn't passed out. 'What a complex scent that flower has. We'll have to get the E-Nose to give us the recipe. Now, what does it remind you of?'

She took an extra big sniff.

'Babies' nappies!' she cried. 'I'm sure they're in there somewhere. Are you getting a whiff?'

'*Mummmm*,' said Juniper, equally excited. 'Isn't it wonderful?'

Kit heard her talking as he hovered outside the door. He groaned.

Maybe, for their first trip out, Gran's Bingo Club was a bit too risky. The big wide world and Juniper would *gradually* get used to each  other. But Kit could see it was going to take time.

'Hey, Juniper, I've been thinking,' he called. 'There's a Museum of Milk-Bottle Tops we could go to. It's only two bus rides away. Yes, honest, it's really popular. All the coolest kids go there!'

# Six weeks later

'Hey, Mr Stinky!' shouted a sneery voice across the schoolyard.

Kit sighed.

He'd thought that, after the summer break, the jokes about his smell would be dead and buried. He was right. Even Laura had got bored with them. But not Sophie. She found them even funnier than before.

'*Phew!*' Sophie started off, holding her nose. 'No one'll sit next to *you*! Not unless Miss gives them a gas mask!'

But strangely Kit didn't feel crushed. He didn't slink away, with his stomach scrunched into knots. Instead, he held his head high.

'You can say anything you like,' he told her. 'It won't make any difference. 'Cos I *know* I don't smell.'

Sophie looked confused for a second. She  hadn't expected this kind of unshakeable self-confidence. What had happened to Kit over the summer holidays?

But she was soon back on the attack.

'You smell like dog poo. Actually, dog poo smells nice compared to you!'

'No, it doesn't,' said Kit, calmly.

'Prove it!' she challenged him, quick as a flash.

'No problem,' shrugged Kit.

He took something out of his pocket. It was a little glass bottle with a silver top.

Sophie stared at it. 'What's that?'

'It's my special, super, anti-smell body spray,' said Kit. 'Even I'm not worried about nasty niffs with this.'

'Let's see that,' said Sophie, grabbing it off him.

'Hey!' said Kit, letting her take it. 'That cost a fortune.'

He moved away. Far, far away.

'You don't need much,' he yelled from a safe distance. 'One good squirt should do it.'

'What's it called, this stuff?' shouted Sophie,

as she started unscrewing the top. 'I mean, it's got a *name*, hasn't it?'

'Oh yes,' Kit murmured to himself as he moved even further off. 'It's got a name. It's called Essence of Titan Arum.'